From the author, MATT SHAW

Author of:

The Big Blue

Below Deck

Below Deck: Mermaids

Mariana Trench

Octopus Trilogy

.

Prologue:

A Brief History of Nessie

'The Loch Ness monster, also known as Nessie. A large marine creature believed, by some, to stalk the waters of Loch Ness, in Scotland.

Over the years, most of the alleged evidence supporting the creature's existence has been debunked. As a result, it is widely believed that the monster is, like Bigfoot, nothing more than a myth.

Reports of Nessie go back hundreds of years. Local stone carvings by the Pict, ancient people who used to live in what is now eastern and northeastern Scotland, even depict a large, mysterious beast with flippers. The first written account, meanwhile, is found in a biography of St. Columba, from 565 AD. Within those pages,

Columba writes about how the monster bit a swimmer. It was about to attack another when Columba intervened, ordering the creature to "go back". To their relief, the beast obeyed and disappeared back into the murky waters. From then, over the centuries, only occasional sightings were reported. Many of the supposed encounters seem heavily inspired by Scottish folklore, which abounds with such water creatures.

1933. The road adjacent to Loch Ness had recently been finished. It offered perfect, unobstructed views of the lake. In April of that year, a couple reportedly saw an enormous animal. When talking to others, recounting what they saw, they compared it to a dragon, or a prehistoric dinosaur. They watched it until it disappeared into the waters once more.

At the time, the papers reported on the sighting. The report encouraged others to step forward if they had seen anything and, as a result, numerous sightings followed.

December of the same year. The newspaper, The Daily Mail, commissioned Marmaduke Wetherell to hunt Nessie. Marmaduke himself was a big-game hunter so if anyone was up for the challenge, it would be him and - sure enough - he soon found large footprints which he reported as belonging to "a very powerful soft-footed animal about 20 feet long." Others were not convinced by what he had seen, and further investigations were made. These investigations, performed by zoologists at the Natural History Museum, determined the tracks were all identical. The cause of the footprints? An umbrella stand, or ashtray that had a hippopotamus leg as a base. The footprints were definitely fake. What was never determined was Wetherell's role in the hoax.

Even so, the news only encouraged others to step forward and try to prove the monster's existence and, in 1934, English physician Robert Kenneth Wilson managed to photograph the sea-serpent. This image became known as the "surgeon's photograph". The picture, appearing to show the monster's small head and neck, was subsequently printed by The Daily Mail which, in turn, sparked an international sensation with many people stating the creature was a plesiosaur; a marine reptile thought to have gone extinct approximately 65 million years ago. This was later debunked too.

In 1987 and 2003, several sonar explorations were undertaken to locate Nessie, but nothing was found. More and more photos came to light, showing the beast, but - again - these were found to be fake. Then, in 1994, Wilson's photograph was also revealed to be an elaborate hoax. In this instance, the "monster" was found to be a plastic-and-wooden head attached to a toy submarine. The hoax itself supposedly spearheaded by Wetherell.

With the advancement of technology and science, further tests were done in 2018. One such test involved conducting a DNA survey of Loch Ness. The reasons for this were to determine what organisms lived in the waters. There were no signs of a plesiosaur. There were no signs of other such large animals either. What they did discover was the presence of numerous eels. Given the longest eel ever recorded measured in at just shy of twenty feet, having been caught in British waters just off Plymouth, it left researchers fairly confident that Nessie *could* be a monster eel. Even so, the legend of Loch Ness remained both popular and profitable and, in the early 21st Century, it was thought to have contributed to almost $80 million, annually, to Scotland's economy.'

Victoria Kneller, soon to be "Dr" if she passed this final paper, took her seat at the large office table, where some of the teaching heads were sitting having listened to her presentation. Whilst she spoke with excitement, and passion - no one else in the room appeared to share such enthusiasm for her talk.

'So, it's an eel,' Victoria's lecturer Dr. Seb Clifton said.

'That's a theory,' Victoria admitted.

'Well it sounds like a concrete one,' Seb said with a cocky laugh and side glance to his colleagues, who he had expected to laugh along. 'DNA doesn't lie. They tested the waters. No dinosaurs. No big beasts. Just eels and little fishies. It doesn't exactly sound like there is much of a mystery to look into anymore.' He laughed again. 'Think if you wanted to jump on that bang-wagon, you needed to be out there, searching around, back in the eighties at minimum.'

Dr. Jeremy Black, the head of the department, leaned forward in his chair. His heavy-set body caused the seat to creak beneath his weight. 'Speaking frankly, it doesn't sound like there is much for you to look at out there. You want to investigate and write a paper on something which has already been investigated and written about numerous times with everyone saying the same thing; the Loch Ness monster does not exist.' He asked, 'Is there a reason why you want to cover this subject for your final paper? Is there not something else you can do?'

'I feel passionate about this.'

Dr. Jeremy Black shrugged. 'Look, we can't tell you what you can and cannot write. It's down to you to study what you want but what we can do is *advise* you. And, we're advising you that this probably won't give you many opportunities to score too highly. I'd recommend perhaps going away for the night and having a think...'

Victoria cut him off and said, 'I have given it a think. This is what I want to write.' She stopped short of saying how she'd already booked herself a quiet cabin on the banks of Loch Ness. She hadn't planned to book the cabin before talking to her tutors but, when she checked the website, it offered her a discount code if she booked there and then. It was too good a deal to turn down. In further defence of her choice, Victoria added, 'Man has studied sharks for a number of years too. There's lots of data about the various species inhabiting the world's oceans. What if I had said I wanted to do a paper on sharks?'

Dr. Seb Clifton laughed again - an irritating trait. He said, 'It helps that sharks actually exist. What you're proposing is going out to do a paper on something which has been proven to not exist. It's hard to write data and such on something which isn't there, is it not?'

'There's always data to be found,' Victoria said, grateful that Dr. Clifton had brought this up. 'The interesting part comes from *what* data is found.'

Dr. Clifton threw his hands up in the air as if to say, *that's it, I give up!* Victoria found it hard to stifle her smile.

'Well…' Dr. Black shrugged again. 'Good luck with your research.'

Victoria smiled again. She knew Dr. Black wasn't being sincere but, she refused to stoop to their levels. Instead, she simply said, 'Thank you.' She just hoped that they wouldn't give her a bad mark for handing the paper in. Not without reading it properly first. If she wrote "crap" then she'd expect a bad mark. That was fair enough. But to get a poorer result because she went against what they had said? That wouldn't be fair.

Victoria stood up and grabbed her jacket from the back of the chair. As she put it on, she couldn't help but think how far she had come since first walking through the university's doors almost four years ago now. One more paper and it could all be done. She would be Dr. Victoria Kneller. Well, so long as she passed. And, admittedly, it didn't mean she could practise medicine but that didn't matter to her. It still sounded cool to be known as "doctor".

With her coat on, she left the room. She knew, the moment the office door closed behind her, they'd be talking about her but - to hell with them. This was a subject she had been passionate about since being a little girl and she knew, whether they believed in her or not, she could turn in a good paper.

Dr. Clifton turned to his colleague and said, 'Please, please, please... If she retakes next year... Put her in someone else's class.'

Dr. Black said nothing. He just watched Victoria walk away, through the glass doors. Whilst he couldn't help but feel this student was making a mistake, so close to the end of the course, he was still impressed with her stubbornness to change, and her passion for the subject. Eventually he quietly said, 'Well, good luck to her.'

Little did either of them know, they wouldn't see her alive again.

* * * * *

Jim Mcleod tossed the small ball for his cocker-spaniel, Casper. The same as every other morning, the pair walked along the shoreline of Loch Ness; Jim's favourite area, if only for the magnificent views stretching before him. It was peaceful and helped calm his everyday stresses, even when Casper always managed to find the muddiest puddle to roll around in.

The ball hit a rock jutting out from the ground and bounced off over towards the cold water's edge. With an enthusiastic bark, up for the chase, Casper ran to the ball only to then run straight past it with his attention pulled elsewhere.

Jim watched as Casper started to dig at something sticking out from the muddy bank. 'What you got, boy?' It was nothing new to see Casper trying to get to something he shouldn't and was only ever a problem when it was something he then tried to eat. Nine times out of ten it was a "more interesting" stick, or something similar. But then, the last thing he needed was a vet's bill because the dumb dog ate something he shouldn't have. 'What is it?' Jim asked again as he walked on up behind his dog. When Casper refused to move, Jim encouraged him out of the way with a gentle foot. Usually, Casper would be quick to move in such circumstances but, whatever this was that he'd found - Casper wanted it. 'Move, boy!' Jim leaned down, just as Casper bit down on whatever it was. 'Give it here,' he said as he fished the mystery item from Casper's mouth; a task easier said than done.

With the item now in his possession, Jim stood up to his full height to take a look at it. Casper sat down in front of his master, hoping that Jim would let him keep whatever it was.

'What we got here then, boy?' Jim froze. It took a couple of seconds to realise what it was but - he was holding a part of a human hand. A thumb, connected to a finger. Nails painted red. The rest of the hand was missing, having been torn away by something. Out of shock, Jim dropped the body part, not that it had a chance to land on the wet ground. Casper caught it and immediately started chewing as Jim scanned the nearby area, wondering if there was anything else. With nothing obvious to be seen, Jim's eyes turned to the vast stretch of water before him. He knew that if there was any more of the body floating around out there, his walks would have to relocate elsewhere. First the police would flock to the area, then the journalists and then the damned tourists. All of them stamping around the place, littering here and there and just creating the level of noise he came here to escape. All he could hope was that nothing else would rise up from the depths; this piece of "evidence" of what had happened being the last of it.

Quietly, Jim said to Casper, 'You get that down you boy. You make it gone.' To his relief, Casper had already swallowed his mouthful. 'Good lad,' Jim said before pushing on with his walk.

When he got home, just as she always did, Jim's wife asked how his walk had gone. He replied, telling her it was pretty much the same as usual.

All being good, nothing else would wash ashore and – tomorrow and the following days - his walk would continue to be undisturbed.

He sighed. 'Just another beautiful day on the banks of...'

LOCH

NESS

Chapter One

'Can you get the door? Steve's here.' Jim's wife, Angie, called out from the kitchen where she was preparing dinner. Out of the kitchen window, she'd seen Officer Steve Chappo pull up in his police car. It was nothing new. Coming from a small village, everyone knew everyone. Steve and Jim were friends, going back a number of years now. Although, in fairness, he didn't tend to show up at their house whilst he was on duty.

Jim got up from his preferred armchair and walked from living room to hallway, mumbling under his breath the whole way. He had literally only *just* sat down. Why was it that whenever he was "needed", it was always when he'd just made himself comfortable? With Angie preparing dinner for them, in the kitchen, he knew better than to pose such a question to her. He could hear her response already, *Oh. I'm sorry. Was your sitting interrupted? Must be nice to be able to sit down, hey big man? Tell you what, you go back and make yourself nice and snug and I'll get the door. Then, I'll fetch you a beer from the fridge and bring it through to you before giving you a foot rub. How's that sound, my darling?*

Jim opened the front door and smiled at his old friend. 'Wasn't expecting to see you today,' Jim said.

'I wasn't expecting to be doing a house visit,' Steve said. He looked over Jim's shoulder and asked, 'Angie home?'

'Aye. She's in the kitchen. Did you need her?'

'No, no. It's you I needed to talk to.'

'Oh?' Jim laughed. 'Sounds very authoritative.'

Steve didn't laugh and, slowly, Jim's smile faded as he came to realise that this wasn't *just* a social visit.

Jim asked, 'What's this about?'

'You want to step out here a minute?' Steve explained, 'Conversation between you and me...'

Jim knew Steve was referring to the possibility of Angie listening in. He nodded and stepped out of the house, pulling the door closed behind him as he did so. He asked again, 'What's this about?'

'How's Casper?'

Jim frowned. Steve didn't usually ask about the well-being of his dog. In fact, when Steve came round, he would more often than not ignore Casper entirely, even when the dopey dog was practically begging him for affection. Jim said, 'He's good.'

'Not got an upset belly?'

'Should he have?'

'Well, it's a possibility.' Steve continued, 'You know, if he has eaten something he shouldn't have.'

Jim continued to play dumb. 'He seems to be fine, thankfully.'

'That's good to hear. Always a terrible shame when something happens to a pet, you know?' Steve paused a moment and then smiled. Jim wasn't stupid. He heard the threat in Steve's tone. Bored with playing games, Steve dropped the act and told him out-right, 'You know the rules. What are you playing at?'

'How did you know?' Jim asked.

'You were seen.'

'I didn't see anyone.'

'Doesn't mean they didn't see you. Thing is, this isn't the first time you've interfered, is it?'

'I'm just doing my part in keeping the place clean.'

'Don't give me that. You know what you're doing.'

'What can I say? I like my walks. I don't want them ruined.'

'Find someplace else to walk.'

'Creature of habit.'

Steve paused, unsure what he could say - or do - to keep his friend in check. 'I'm just trying to look out for you,' he eventually said.

'And I appreciate that.'

'Others…'

'Others?'

'They've had enough.'

'And I'm sorry about that.'

The pair just stood a moment, in silence. Jim could see from Steve's face that there was more conversation to be had. He cut to the chase and asked, 'So, what else can I do for you?'

Steve went to say something before he stopped himself. He thought for a moment and realised he had no choice but to spit out what needed to be said. With a sharp intake of breath, and ready for a fight, he said, 'I got to take Casper.'

'What?!'

'That's what they said. We need to get the people talking again and, unfortunately, you stopped that from happening on your morning walk - and not for the first time.' He said again, 'I got to take the dog. Don't make this any harder than it already is, Jim.'

'You're not taking my dog.'

Steve nodded. 'Yes, I am. If it stops you from...'

'Okay I'm sorry. I saw… What was left. I remem-bered how busy it gets down there after a fresh sighting and… I wasn't thinking.'

Steve corrected him, 'You weren't thinking of anyone but yourself.' He continued, 'Changes nothing. They've had enough of your ways. I got to take the dog.'

'What if I suggest another way?'

Chapter Two

'Anything I would have heard of?' Lily asked.

Lily Briers, twenty-four years old, worked in a small hotel close to Loch Ness. It wasn't the best of jobs but, it paid the bills and kept her local enough to check in on her ageing parents whenever she wanted.

Lily was checking in the latest guest - the *only* guest for the day to be doing so. His name was Reece Walker and, just as he told everyone, he'd "accidentally" let slip that he was in town to write a book. That led to telling Lily that he was an author which, in turn, drew her question, *anything I would have heard of*.

Reece smiled. 'I doubt it,' he said. He wasn't being modest. Reece hadn't had a successful book in over ten years now, much to the frustration of his agent. The agency had been very clear that, if he didn't have one soon, he would be dropped from *their* books. Within a week, he approached them about his new book - a monster book, based on the legend of Loch Ness. Whilst he was enthusiastic about it, having always been fascinated by the alleged sightings of a potential dinosaur, he knew that the stories were bullshit. But that didn't mean they couldn't lead to him writing a story that his readers - and *new* readers, hopefully - *wouldn't* regard as "bullshit".

'So, what brings you out here?' Lily asked. 'You writing a book about our little lake monster?'

Reece laughed. 'I was toying with the idea.'

Lily smiled. 'You certainly wouldn't be the first.' She continued, 'Seems like most months we have someone coming by here, thinking they're going to be writing the next best lake monster book. Either that or it's filmmakers wanting to turn our Nessie into something fit for the silver screen… Or documentary crews and scientists looking to capture something no one else has yet seen.'

28

Reece couldn't help but to notice, 'You don't sound very impressed.'

'Are you kidding? Nessie keeps the roof over our head and the bills paid. We welcome anyone and everyone. It would just be nice to have an original story once in a while.' With that, she asked, 'So, tell me Mr. Walker, what's your Nessie going to be about?'

Reece smiled. 'Sorry. Spoilers and all that.' The truth of the matter was, he had no idea what his story was going to be about yet. He just knew he wanted to use Loch Ness as the setting. He figured he would come up here for a couple of weeks, take in the sights and - just - explore. In doing so, he hoped the story would come to mind as was often the case when he went off exploring the country.

'Do I at least get a signed copy when you've finished it?' Lily asked with a teasing smile on her cute face. Reece couldn't help but think she was flirting with him, despite the twenty-year age difference. Given how his wife had left him after the last booked flopped and he had turned to alcohol to cheer himself up, it was nice to feel wanted by someone again, even if there was a part of him which was constantly reminding him that *she's doing her job*.

'We'll have to see,' he said. That was his way of saying "no" without actually upsetting whoever was on the receiving end of it. Had his last few books not bombed, he might have been more inclined to give a copy away for free, especially if it could potentially lead on to something as sweet as getting his nuts sucked. As it was, he needed all the sales he could get. So, if she was curious about it, she could buy her own and help him look "good" to his agents again.

'Can you at least make me a character in the book?'

Reece looked at her name badge; first name only. 'Lily?'

Lily nodded. 'Briers. That's B-R-I-E-R-S.'

Reece couldn't help but laugh. Whether she was being serious or not, he liked her confidence. 'I can probably do that,' he said.

Just as her previous request hadn't been the first time he had been asked for a signed book, this wasn't the first time he had been asked to turn someone into a character either. Depending on the name and the book being written, he didn't usually mind doing this for people because it meant they were more inclined to buy the book. Most of them wouldn't read it but they would show it to their friends. *Here, this is me.*

Reece realised this was a pretty one-sided conversation, what with her demands, so - now he had agreed to something for her - he decided it was time to get something for himself. 'Question is, if I am naming a character after you…'

'A cute, fun-loving one,' Lily was quick to say.

'Okay… If I am naming a cute, fun-loving character after you… Does that mean I get a free room upgrade? Or maybe breakfast included?'

Lily smiled. She held out a room key and said, 'You'll have to see for yourself.'

Chapter Three

For unobstructed views of the Loch, the website listing
the hotel's rooms charged extra. Whilst Reece hated the
way companies always found extra ways of getting
money out of people, he paid the additional monies because he knew it would be worthwhile in this instance.
In his head, he had envisioned pulling the room's small
table away from the corner and pushing it up against the
window. Then, on the rainy days, he'd be able to sit at
the desk, laptop open, and just stare out to the Loch.
This way, he still had the inspiration he was looking for
but, he was also warm. Better yet, the website boasted
the hotel's excellent room service so he'd be both warm

and a phone call away from good food and booze. Except…

Reece put his bags down on the bed and looked out of the window with a less than impressed look on his face. The unobstructed views of the Loch were actually unobstructed views of the hotel's ugly-looking car park. This wasn't an upgrade. This was a downgrade.

Frustrated he'd paid for something he'd not received, he grabbed the phone from the bedside table and called down to the reception desk.

Within a few rings, a male voice answered, 'Front desk.'

'Hi, this is Mr. Walker. I just checked into room 32.' Reece continued, 'When I put my details in online, I paid extra for views of the loch but…'

'I'm terribly sorry, sir, we don't have availability in those rooms as of right now.'

'But I pre-booked it.'

'All rooms are subject to availability. I'm sorry about that…'

'But the receipt I got clearly shows I've been billed for the more expensive room.' Despite the "apology" coming from the voice on the other end of the phone, Reece couldn't help but feel his temper start to build. He'd paid extra for the room. He had pre-booked it. The website showed availability. Now there was none, apparently, and yet - they'd not only *not* told him this on check-in but they also charged him the same amount. From where he was standing - in his shitty room with the shittier view - he couldn't help but feel this was all a scam. 'How many other customers do you do this too?' Reece asked.

'What do you mean, sir?'

'You charge them for the more expensive room and then put them in one of the others. How many other people do you do that too, hoping they won't say anything or - if they do - that they won't notice you still billed them the same.'

'That was an oversight, sir. We can - and will - refund the difference for you immediately.'

'Oh? It's immediately going to go on my card, is it?'

'It will take about five to seven days to clear, sir, but that...'

'Yeah, yeah... Just put the refund through, please. I'll pop across for a receipt when I head out.' Reece had heard enough bullshit. He knew the guy on the phone was going to blame the banks for the tardiness of the money going back into his account and - there was just something about this prick's voice which made Reece feel angrier than was probably necessary. Hanging up on him might have felt rude but, it was the safest option. At least this way he wasn't going to get kicked out for being unnecessarily aggressive, even if he felt the idiot did deserve it.

Reece walked back over to the window and stared out towards the grey car park. It wasn't ideal but, at the end of the day, he was still close enough to the Loch that he could walk down to it and go exploring and *that* was the real purpose of booking this place. He smiled as - still staring out of the window - he imagined a part in his book which could have the Loch Ness monster slither from the murky waters and into this car park. He'd write about a snotty-shit of a bellboy walking out of the hotel only to get ripped apart by the monster's razor-sharp teeth and, his innards licked out by the snake-like tongue. As his imagination continued to get the better of him, Reece couldn't help but to laugh. 'Yeah, that's probably a bit too far even for my readers.' He already knew he was going to be fighting a battle with the release of this book and the feelings of any Scot who happened to read it. No doubt he'd get crap for misrepresenting their people or their ways or writing about Nessie in an unbelievable manner but - whatever. His books were never supposed to be about realism. They were supposed to be fun; a little light entertainment to pass the hours away. Reece closed his eyes for a moment and tried to silence his brain as it started to race in the direction of some of the reviews he'd already received for his work. People who had taken his work way too seriously and, essentially, lynched him on Amazon, stating that a child could write better. With a new book to write, he didn't need to be thinking about those stuck-up pricks just yet. Especially seeing as, so far, he had written zero words for the new story. This was - and always has been - the worst part of writing; the initial blank pages taunting him with how pristine and untouched they were.

'Fuck it,' he muttered as he turned and left the room. With his brain still screaming its frustration towards the one-star reviews he'd received, he figured now was *not* the time to break out his MacBook Pro to start writing. Instead, he'd go for the first of many anticipated walks across to the loch. Besides which, it made sense to do that now seeing as Scotland was known for its rain and - currently - it was fairly bright out there.

Chapter Four

There was no hiding the surprise on Reece's face when
he saw the crowd of people gathered around the reception desk once the elevator doors opened. He stepped
out into the narrow foyer and watched - with some
amusement - as a male member of staff struggled to
maintain control of the people shouting to book the last
of the rooms. In his mind, Reece had already decided
the guy behind the desk was the same prick he'd spoken
to on the phone so, he was happy to see him stressed.
They called that "Karma", he though.

As he started down the foyer, towards the main entrance of the hotel, Lily almost bumped into him as she
came from one of the side rooms. With the reception
desk struggling to cope, she had been called off her

break to lend a hand with a promise that, she could go back on her break once the crowd was dealt with.

'So what happened to my upgrade?' Reece asked as they continued down the foyer together.

'How do you know that room wasn't the best of what we had available?'

'So these people won't get a better room than the cupboard you gave me?'

Lily laughed. 'Most of these people will be turned away, just as anyone else will be when they come too. At least you have a room. In fact, we could have probably charged you *more*.'

'Technically you did,' Reece said. 'You know, seeing as I paid for a room upgrade I didn't receive.'

Lily laughed. 'Whoops.'

'Yeah. Whoops.' Reece continued, 'Just so you know, I've decided about your character. Turns out, she isn't that nice and - sorry to say - she isn't that cute either.'

'Ah don't be like that,' Lily said. 'Anyway, I would have thought you'd have been happy.'

39

'At being ripped off?'

'No. About the news.'

'The news?'

'You don't know?'

'You're talking in riddles,' Reece said.

'Let's just say, none of these people have pre-booked. They've all just flocked here on the off-chance we have space, just so they can be as close to the Loch as possible.' As Lily stepped behind the counter, she flashed Reece a smile and said, 'Looks like Nessie has popped up to say hello. Must have known you were writing a book about her.'

Reece's heart skipped a beat. *A sighting of the elusive creature just as he happened to show up?* Perfect timing, he thought. He looked around at the people, frantically trying to get a room. These weren't holiday-makers, or people passing through on a business trip. They were journalists, desperate to get a room so they could be local to the breaking story.

Reece hurried from the hotel. He was shocked to see the full carpark outside, and the fact that more cars were circling it, as the drivers tried to find a space for themselves.

* * * * *

The hotel was situated on the banks of Loch Ness. With exceptional ratings, it was considered one of the best in the area. It helped that it was also the most local to where the Loch Ness monster was usually sighted too. Desperate monster-hunters would travel from far and wide to stay here, in the hope of getting a glimpse of the elusive creature for themselves.

It always made Reece laugh whenever he heard about such people venturing out here, or to other places in the world which had myths of their own. It didn't matter how many scientists stepped forward to prove Nessie wasn't real, people were *still* willing to believe. It made Reece laugh more because, at the same time, scientists were warning people there was a killer virus out there, infecting millions of people across the world, and yet people refused to believe them either. In short - what good were "scientists" when the general public chose to believe in what *they* wanted to believe and not what the facts pointed to. Still, that was humanity in a nutshell, *fucking retarded*. If someone said one thing, there'd always be someone close by to say that they're wrong.

'Sorry, you can't go down there,' a voice shouted over to Reece as he started down towards the Loch.

Reece turned and saw a policeman walking towards him, along with another office. 'Worried the monster is going to get me?' Reece laughed.

The officers didn't find him funny. They passed Reece and started to stretch out police tape to corner off the area.

'You're being serious? I can't go down to the water's edge?' Reece realised this wasn't a standard sighting of the Loch Ness monster. If it were, people would flock to try and see it for themselves, just as they sometimes did, but the police wouldn't come down and tape the area off. 'What's going on?' he asked.

'Sorry, sir, we're going to have to ask you to step away now.'

Before Reece could ask anything else, or even get an answer to his original question, the first of the journalists appeared next to him. Immediately, they started asking questions of their own, 'What can you tell us about the body? Have you managed to ID them yet?'

'The body?' Reece said, genuinely surprised. 'I thought there had been a sighting of Nessie?' The journalist ignored him, as though Reece wasn't even standing next to him. Confused, but knowing he wasn't going to get any answers, Reece turned away and made his way back to the hotel.

As he crossed the carpark, more journalists passed by him. They too were heading to where the other journalist was standing. Each of them, desperate for the scoop -though Reece could have saved them the time - none of them were going to be getting the answers from *those* officers.

Chapter Five

Daylight had faded to night. Reece was still sitting in the bar, propped up at the bar itself where he had set up "base camp" for himself. In front of his placing, there was a glass of vodka and orange. To the side of that was his closed notebook and his cheap pen. The barstool he had chosen for himself was the closest one to the television set which, after talking to the bartender, was showing the local news-station.

Reece had decided the bar would be the best place to spend his day. Not only did it mean he could drink without having to pay a surcharge each time he wanted alcohol delivered to his room, but it also meant he was within ear-shot of other patrons - all of whom, as expected, were discussing the day's events.

In truth, what was happening out there didn't impact Reece at all. He was there to write a fictional story about the monster. The fact there'd been an "incident" was just good timing for him. He could watch how it was handled, listen to how people spoke and just soak in the atmosphere; all of which would help make his story more realistic, even if it was primarily fiction it was still good to have some realism within.

'Here we go,' the bartender said as he poured out a pint for another hotel guest. His eyes were glued to the television set to such an extent that he accidentally over-poured the beer. He stopped pouring, set the beer down and wiped his hand clean, all the time not taking his eyes from what was being reported on-screen.

Reece was watching the news too. They were playing drone footage of the Loch and, when the hotel came into view, there was a little cheer from some of the patrons which amused Reece up until the point the bartender hushed everyone. He turned the volume up on the controller.

'... The identity of the woman has yet to be released but, from what we are hearing, she was a local lady known around the community.'

The drone footage cut back to the studios. 'Again, this just in, a female body has been found on the banks of Loch Ness. According to one eye-witness report; the woman, in her fifties, was believed to have been out walking her dog when she was attacked - and killed - by an unknown creature which came up out of the loch in, what is being described as, "a frenzied attack". The news anchor promised, 'We will bring you more of this story as it unfolds.' She carried on speaking, 'In the meantime, a record number of...' The bartender turned the television back down.

Reece had expected a shocked hush around the bar. It had finally been confirmed that there *was* a body out there and, on any day of the week, it was always sad when someone had lost their life. Yet, people were talking in hushed, yet excited, whispers. They were questioning whether it had been Nessie. The first time in recent history that the creature had come up out of the water.

The bartender made a flippant remark to his colleague who was standing a few feet away, 'Well, guess we're about to get busy again.'

His colleague responded with a laugh and, 'So long as they tip well.'

'Everyone wants to see our Nessie,' the bartender said.

Reece couldn't help but to ask him, 'Is there anything out there which could attack a person?'

'Aye. Nessie. You heard it here first.'

'Anything that's proven to actually exist?' Reece asked sarcastically.

The bartender leaned forward on the bar and spoke in a hushed voice. Quietly, he said, 'There's the Scottish wildcat. Very rare. In fact, they think there's only about 35 left in the wild now but… If cornered… Could tear a man to pieces in the blink of an eye. Very aggressive.'

'Oh really?' Reece didn't much study nature. Had he done so, he would have known the bartender was mocking him for, in reality, the Scottish wildcat certainly wouldn't kill a person. Whilst it was vicious to its prey and known for being untameable - they spent more time running from humans than stalking them.

'You see one of those out there and you just do yourself a favour,' the man continued, 'and don't move.'

The bartender's colleague couldn't help but to laugh as he overheard the conversation. Had he not done so, Reece probably would have left the bar believing everything he'd heard. As it was, he just shook his head as, finally, the bartender started to laugh too.

The bartender admitted, 'Not much out there could tear a person to pieces. Elk, wildcat, badgers… Certainly not big cats or bears so… If whatever did that to the woman was an animal… It's new to us.' Before he could say anything else, the bartender was called away to the other end of the bar, by someone else waiting for service.

Reece sat there a moment with his imagination in overdrive. He knew the chances of Nessie actually existing - at least in the sea-serpent form that most people knew her as - were slim to none and yet, he still had that "what if" feeling in the forefront of his mind. Along with that, there was a little bubble of excitement in the pit of his stomach; something not experienced for many years now. The sea-monster might not live, swimming in the murky depths only to occasionally surface, but - what if there were *other* creatures down there? What if today was the first day they were making themselves known?

Keen to get back to his room, and up to his waiting laptop, Reece downed the last of his drink. He ordered another to take up with him and, fresh drink in hand, he headed to his room.

Chapter One

Mary Kiefel stood at the water's edge. Her pet dog, a black Labrador named Banksy, was sniffing around in the nearby muddy sands. Its tail wagged with happiness, just as it always did when she brought it out this way for a walk; something which she tried to do at least once a week, depending on the weather.

It was early morning. It wasn't raining, nor was it scheduled to rain according to the weather reports, but the clouds above made sure as to block out the sun and darken the miserable landscape. A shame as, on a bright sunny day, it looked truly spectacular down by the Loch, no matter which part you stood at.

Mary didn't mind the darkness. She would have preferred a bright day - who wouldn't? - but it wasn't raining and it wasn't too chilly so, really, what was there to complain about? Also - another reason she liked it down here - it was an escape from the city, and her office. With how stressful her work had been recently, that could only have been a good thing.

Mary was staring out into the vast waters. Occasionally a little fish would jump up, out of the water, to snatch a low-flying insect from the air. When it landed back in the water - there was barely a ripple.

Something else was nicer about being out here too; the air was cleaner. Keen to clear out her city-damaged lungs, Mary sucked in a deep lungful of this fresher air. She held it there for a moment and - then - slowly exhaled. In an ideal world she would move out here, just to get away from the hustle and bustle of the city. Sure, she would have to go back there on a daily basis, unless the office permitted her to work from home instead, but that wouldn't have been a problem. At the end of the day,

she still would have come back out to the relaxing sur-
roundings of the countryside. As it was, she'd just go
home to her small apartment and sit there, listening to
neighbours screaming and noisy traffic outside. She
sighed with disappointment as her she remembered *that*
was what was waiting for her back home, when she and
Banksy were ready to leave.

It was nice to dream - such as dreaming about moving
out to the country - but, at the same time, it was also a
little depressing when the realisation hit home about the
chances of actually turning that dream into a reality.
When Mary thought about it further, she questioned
whether it *was* actually "nice" to dream. Given the disappointment that followed, when said dreams weren't
realised, perhaps it was better to just turn a person's
mind off from that kind of thing? Just - she told herself -
be content with what you have and…

The water in front of her rippled, distracting her from
her thoughts as her eyes fixed to where it had happened.
Must have been a bigger fish, she told herself. She

watched for a moment longer, curious as to see whether it would appear again but - nothing.

Banksy barked from a few feet away, which visibly startled Mary. She laughed at herself, 'Stupid bitch!' as she turned to see what Banksy had found. She'd expected to see him standing there, staring at whatever he'd dug up but - instead - he was looking right back at Mary with his head tilted to the side.

Mary said, 'Scared me, dumb dog.'

Banksy whined and laid down submissively.

'Oh I didn't mean it,' Mary said. 'There's no need to be so melodramatic.' But Banksy wasn't reacting to Mary calling him a "dumb dog". He was reacting to what had quietly surfaced from the water directly behind Mary.

Chapter Two

Banksy stood his ground and barked loudly right up until the moment Mary's pained scream was cut short. As soon as she fell silent, Banksy did too. More than that, he turned and ran off into the nearby woodlands. Mary, on the other hand, just stood there a moment with a look of both shock and fear on her face. She blinked a couple of times and then, slowly, looked down to her stomach. Her top had been ripped open, as had her flesh beneath. Unsure of how bad the wound was, she lifted her top in time to see her warm intestines slip out and splatter onto the wet ground at her feet. The blood instantly soaked into the hungry earth as, a few feet away and still standing ankle deep in the Loch's cold waters, the attacking creature made a clicking noise from the back of its throat. Mary looked up. The creature tilted its head as it remained staring at Mary, waiting for the last ebb of life to slip away from her.

It didn't have long to wait.

Mary dropped to her knees first and then, a moment later, fell face first into the mud. Behind the creature, ripples appeared on the surface of the water. They were followed by the appearance of more creatures, similar to the one which had killed Mary. Half-reptilian and half-human; green-scaled skin, beady yellow eyes, teeth as sharp as piranha. The creatures stood like man. On the end of their elongated fingers - pin-sharp nails, perfect for ripping into the flesh of their prey.

"Speaking" in a series of clicks, a language never before heard by man, the creatures stretched their grasping hands towards where Mary lay. With her body firmly in their grip, they slowly pulled her into the waters. From there, they'd take her to the deepest depths and - away from prying eyes - they'd feast upon the flesh before the rot kicked in.

One by one, they disappeared beneath the surface - not even leaving a ripple of evidence behind.

Banksy, oblivious to all but the attack, continued to run through the woodlands. In a panic, he had no idea where he was going. *He just knew, he had to get away from there and then Lily popped up and shot him with a twelve-bore shotgun. The force of the round took poor Banksy's fucking head clean off* and 'FUCK SAKE!'

Chapter Six

Reece sat back in the uncomfortable chair which had been provided with his room. His laptop was open in front of him, loaded up onto the Mac program, *PAGES*. Written within the program? The first two chapters of his Loch Ness story. Or rather…

Reece deleted the entire document.

The first two chapters *had* been written within the document. He stood up from the chair and stretched out his back. He'd only been sitting there for a couple of hours now and his back was killing him due to how crap the seating was. Although, to be fair, most hotels had shit seats in them; just something cheap for if needed. They probably don't expect people to be checking in and spending hours and hours sitting away in their rooms.

Reece sighed as he checked the time on his watch. A couple of hours, and fuck all to show for it. From the table, his near empty glass of vodka orange caught his attention. It was safe to safe, whilst he craved another, he'd probably had enough to drink. He'd *certainly* had enough to drink if he was planning on getting any writing done. Good writing, at least.

Fucking fish people? He laughed at where his half-drunk imagination had taken him. *Fucking fish people*? The last thing people would want, when looking for a book on the Loch Ness monster, was a story about these half-human-half-fish things living within the Loch's depths. It was ridiculous, even by his standards. Even if it wasn't, and he had come up with the best story out there, the readers still wouldn't have been happy about reading such trash. Not when they wanted the Loch Ness monster! Maybe if he renamed the book "Fish People of the Deep", or something similar but… Those people buying a book hinting at Nessie would *want* Nessie.

Reece walked over to the window and stared down to the carpark below. As he watched the world go by, he couldn't help but wonder whether this was all a mistake. He loved the idea of there being an actual monster lurking in the deep waters of Loch Ness. He'd been fascinated with it ever since he first heard about it as a young boy. As a result, he had always promised himself to write a fitting story for it but, what if there *was* no fitting story? So many people had stories of their own, based around the myth; some published, some filmed and some just whispered around campfires late at night. Did the world really *want* another story based on it? If they did, they wouldn't want it pointing to a different monster out there. They'd want it traditional. But then, keeping things "traditional" means - it's a story that has been told time and time again and… Books told before, and by far better authors in some instances, don't sell!

He muttered to himself, 'What the fuck are you doing?' He glanced back to his near-finished drink. 'Getting another drink is what you're doing.'

Knowing full well he wasn't going to get any "good" writing done that day, Reece grabbed his jacket and headed back down to the bar. With any luck there'd be something happening down there which could distract him from his writing-woes. Fuck it, even if there wasn't, he knew he could just sit there and look sorry for himself whilst staring at the bottom of yet another glass of alcohol. Sure, he was technically supposed to be working at - at the same time - this was the closest he'd had to a holiday for a while now. *Might as well push the boat out and have a few more drinks*, he thought.

* * * * *

The elevator doors opened and Reece stepped out into the foyer once more. A far cry from earlier, this time it was practically empty, bar the odd hotel guest. Even the reception area was free from staff; no doubt they were taking a moment to have a quick break after the earlier rush, Reece thought.

Reece made his way down the narrow foyer towards where the bar was situated, only to find that the doors were closed. Not just that, it looked pretty damn dark through the glass windows too but then, he figured it was just special glass: You could look out but not see inside.

Reece pushed the left-hand door first but, it didn't budge. He took hold of the handle and pulled but - again - nothing. He tried the right-hand side and - the same.

'They're shut,' a voice said from behind.

Reece about turned. There was a guest standing over by the reception desk. 'Any idea when they'll be opening again?'

The guest shrugged. 'Your guess is as good as mine. Been on the road for the last three hours and want some food.' He explained, 'Just trying to find out now but,' he looked around the reception area, 'seems they're shut too!'

Unsure whether he'd somehow lost time somewhere, Reece checked his watch. It was a little after seven. He had known hotel bars close early before but, never at *this* time.

'I'm sure they'll be back soon,' he said, although he didn't exactly sound confident in his thoughts.

'Hope so. Fucking starving,' the guest moaned.

Reece couldn't help but wonder how the hotel had received so many glowing reviews when, really, from the moment he got there it had seemed undeserved of all of them. He gave one final check of the doors to see if they'd somehow magically unlocked themselves. They hadn't.

Reece headed back to his "cell" wondering why the hell he wasn't writing a book based on the *Bermuda Triangle* instead. At least it would have been warmer out there, doing his "research".

Chapter Seven

The local government bodies were sitting up on the town hall's small stage. Alongside them, Steve Chappo was standing - talking to the locals who'd come along to the scheduled meeting.

'Now I know some of you wanted us to use Jim Mcleod's dog to get the attention but Jim has given us his assurances he won't interfere with any future plans.'

'He said that last time,' a voice called out from the seated crowd.

Steve continued, 'And to make amends this time, he did freely volunteer his wife to us so... Let bygones be bygones and, let us give thanks to Jim for his generous donation to the cause.' Steve turned his body in Jim's direction and started to applaud. Others around the room joined him in the applause.

Jim put his hand up as if to say, *Not a problem.*

'And,' Steve added, 'we would also like to take a moment to give commiserations for your loss. Angie was a,' he hesitated a moment as he searched the right words, '*fine* woman.'

Jim laughed. 'Fine? She was a pain in my arse. I tell you; I'll live a longer life without her, that much is sure.' There was a nervous ripple of laughter around the room with people unsure as to whether they should laugh at Jim's comments. 'But,' he continued, 'you're very welcome and I am glad I could play my part in helping our fine country out.'

Deep down Jim wasn't "glad" about anything. He knew that, for the foreseeable future, his dog walks were going to be ruined by people searching for the Loch Ness monster. They'd get in his way, they'd stop him and ask him stupid fucking questions - like whether he had seen Nessie for himself; a comment which *used* to get the response, *I wake up with her every morning*. He couldn't say that now that he'd be waking up alone. Still, Jim was fine to "play happy" if it meant they stayed well away from his dog.

Steve turned his body back so that it was pointed right up the middle of the entire congregation. He was, once again, addressing all in the room. 'The good news is we've already had word that the majority of hotels are fully booked for the next two weeks, which was antici-pated although - if being honest - not quite as good as the last time there was a sighting but, early days. We're sure the numbers and bookings will continue to rise and, if they do happen to struggle, we always have a little more of Angie that we can spread around to ensure in-terest remains.'

Angie's body was hidden within the hospital morgue. It wasn't locked in one of the fridges to help keep the freshness. It was left out, locked in a back room so that it could rot as though it were still lying undiscovered outside. Given the nature of what they were saying killed her, it wouldn't have made sense to throw the entire mangled body out in one go. It was much more resourceful to keep bits to scatter around later, just to keep people talking.

Steve continued, 'With the sudden rush of business heading our way over the coming weeks, I hope stock levels have been increased for more merchandise. I appreciate we've taken a different route with this sighting but, let's keep everything tasteful and kid-friendly, okay? Death brings the curious parents flocking but tends to scare the children away. So we don't want to be seeing teddy bears of Nessie with razor-sharp teeth and red eyes, even if they do glow in the dark…' He turned to one of the women sitting close to the front row and - as an aside - said to her, 'Yes, I did see the designs you did, no they're not appropriate. Neither do we want action figures of Angie which come apart at the middle, even if teenagers would appreciate it. Let's keep it decent, folks.' Steve addressed the rest of the room, 'Now, questions will be asked. Everyone was warned about that before we went down this path to get tourism levels back to what they were pre-covid lockdown but, as stated before, there is nothing for anyone to worry about. As explained, just play dumb and direct them to the law enforcement, or hospital. We have all the answers for the questions they could possibly ask and, if they ask something we *can't* answer...' Steve smiled. 'I'm afraid it is an ongoing investigation so we can't comment on that.' The audience laughed. Steve turned to one the local cabinet members and, in a lower voice, said, 'I think that's pretty much everything. Was there anything you wanted to add?'

The man's name was Mark Flemmich. He'd been a voice for the Scottish people for *years* now and, with most people too scared to talk back to him given his fierce reputation as being an argumentative arsehole. Sometimes it was just easier to say nothing and hope he'd change his mind if he raised an idea that no one liked. *This*, letting Nessie kill a person, had been his idea.

Mark stood up and walked over to where Steve was standing. He had just been waiting for *his* turn to say something; anything to be in the limelight. He said, 'I just want to say thank you for playing your part in this. I know it was a shame, having to lose one of our own but… Well… The original plan didn't quite work out, did it?' He shot Jim a look. The original plan was to lose "yet another researcher" - someone the locals wouldn't have cared about as, whenever one scientist disappeared - another would soon appear. 'As Mr. Chappo said, hotel booking are on the rise and we're expecting quite the footfall over the coming weeks so, all being good, everyone should see an increase in their businesses again.' He smiled. 'Then, we can look at raising the taxes you pay, hey?' The government bodies sitting to the side laughed. The audience didn't. Mark was quick to ease their minds and added, 'Do not worry, I jest. About the taxes at least. I'm as serious as a heart attack when I say that this is the best for all of our businesses though so - again - thank you for playing your part.' He turned

69

to Jim and said, 'And although you brought it upon yourself, thank *you* for your contribution to the scheme.'

'You're welcome,' Jim said with a forced smile on his face. There was nothing he wanted more than to smack this prick in the mouth but, he knew it would only get him arrested. Again.

'Anyway, unless anyone has any questions or concerns for us to address, I think that is pretty much everything we have right now.' Mark paused a moment, half-expecting *someone* to pipe up with something. To his relief, given he wanted to get home to watch a program about antiques, the room remained silent. 'That's great.' He quickly said, 'Now I think it would be a good idea to meet in two weeks so we can discuss figures and take a look at how things are going. All being well and good, we can just coast along on this for a good few months before we need to do anything again but - better to be safe.' He turned to Steve and asked, 'Agreed?' Steve nodded. 'So - two weeks today. Same time. Other than that, please travel safe.' He gestured towards the doors before turning away and walking off the stage, in the opposite direction from the "normal" people. Steve just stood there, centre-stage, with his eyes fixed to the back row.

Lily was sitting there, staring right back at him. She bit her bottom lip as she twirled her long hair around her finger playfully. It was a look which made Steve blush. He knew what she wanted. It was the same as what she *always* wanted.

Chapter Eight

Lily screamed, 'Fuck me!' Her hands were cuffed behind her back and she was bent over the bonnet of the police car with her panties pulled to the side and her skirt hitched up.

Steve was standing behind her, his shorts and trousers pulled down to his knees and his arse exposed to the pale moonlight as he thrust in and out of Lily, bareback. One hand had a firm grip of her hair and the other was pressing down on her back, keeping her in place - not that she was trying to get away.

'Cum in me!' she demanded just as Steve's breathing started to become more erratic. 'Give it to me…'

Steve let out a loud sigh as he ejaculated a thick stream of hot semen straight up into Lily's pussy. Given the fact he was married, usually he'd pull out and splash over her arse but - on occasion, the temptation and pleasure were just too much to ignore. This was one such time.

Steve paused there a moment; his prick deep inside her. Enjoying the feeling of having him inside her, Lily clenched her pussy muscles around his shaft, ensuring every last drop of semen was drained from his near-empty sack. She giggled. 'Mmmmm.'

'Tell me about it,' he said. 'I needed that.' He pulled out and pulled his shorts and trousers back up before fastening his belt. Only then did he fish the handcuff keys from his pocket and undo the restraints.

Lily didn't move. She stayed over the bonnet and just enjoyed the sensation of feeling him trickle out and run down the inside of her thigh. *A dirty slut, used and abused just how she liked it.*

'You needed that?' she asked. Then, if only for a pointed dig, she asked, 'Wife not getting the same treatment back home then?'

'I told you before,' Steve snapped, 'we don't discuss my wife.'

'What's the matter? Feeling guilty?' Lily shot straight back. She always liked to wind Steve up about his wife and, despite how moody he could get about it, he didn't really have a leg to stand on. How could he after he'd shot his load up inside *another* woman? 'From that reaction it's fair to say you haven't told her about us yet?' She continued, 'You know, like you promised to do so over a year ago?'

'I told you, now isn't the right time.'

'No, it never is.' Lily adjusted her panties. The last of Steve's semen dribbled out of her and into the gusset of them. *Something for her OnlyFans subscribers to purchase*. She stood up straight and pulled her skirt down, covering herself up. 'Starting to feel like there'll never be a "right" time to tell her.'

'You know it isn't just as easy as telling her? There's a lot to take into consideration.'

'Oh I know. For example, at the moment I'm considering whether we're going anywhere or whether I am better off cutting my losses and finding someone else.' Lily pointed out, 'I'm worth more than being someone's side-dish.'

Steve laughed. 'Someone else? Who else are you going to have around here? Pretty sure you'd tried most of the men around here already. They didn't exactly work out, did they.' He laughed again.

'Fuck you. Why do you think I work in the hotel?' She teased him, 'Checking in all these guests... Meeting new, handsome people on a daily basis.'

'That right?'

'Yep. Especially now Nessie's back in fashion.'

'Uh huh.'

'Only this morning did I check in a very handsome man. A best-selling author too. Sure, he could give me a better life than what you could offer. Probably a better fuck too, given his imagination...'

Steve refused to bite. 'If that's what you want.' He asked, 'So you got his number already, huh?'

'Not yet but wouldn't be hard to get it off the system.'

'So you can't call him now? Shame.'

'Why would I call him now?'

'So you can get him to pick you up,' Steve said.

Steve winked at her before he walked round to the driver's side of the car. He climbed in and locked the door as Lily made her way to the passenger side. She pulled on the handle.

'Seriously?'

Steve laughed as he started the engine to his police car. He put the car in reverse and started backing away, back down the dirt track they'd come up for their secret fuck.

'Are you fucking kidding me?' Lily shouted.

Steve slammed on the brakes and the car skidded to a stop. Lily walked over to the vehicle - passenger side again - and tried the handle for a second time. Still locked.

Steve laughed before he leaned forward and unlocked the door for her. Lily climbed in and slammed the door shut behind her.

'You're an arsehole,' she said.

'And you're mine.' He smiled at her. 'So now we both know where we stand, hey.' He put the car back into reverse and continued down the dirt-track as Lily just sat there, staring out of the window. As he pulled out onto the main road, Steve paused a moment and told her, 'I will tell her. I promise. Just…'

Before he could finish his sentence, Lily said, 'Now isn't a good time. Yeah, yeah…' It would take more than words. He'd been spitting words for too long now and, with the exception of how he fucked, Lily just wasn't impressed anymore. She turned her attention back to the eerily still waters of the loch. Not for the first time in her life, she found herself thinking about just stripping off and walking into the water. She wouldn't stop, she'd just keep going until she was fully submerged. She wouldn't stop… She'd just keep walking until her body gave out and the water drowned her.

Chapter One (take 2)

The water looked black at night. Standing on the shores, watching from the side-lines, a person could think it looked peaceful. Some might have a wish to relocate their lives there, thinking it was a better life. As with most things in life, looks could be deceiving.

Beneath the surface, way down in the darkest depths of the loch, Mary's body had been wedged between some rocks to save it from resurfacing again. Her eyes were wide open, locked in place, but saw nothing anymore. If they were still capable of sight, they'd have seen fish of all sizes feeding upon the various rips in her flesh. Those cold, dead eyes would see larger shapes less than a hundred yards away. Slow, hungry, cautious as those same shapes inched closer, ready for their fill of flesh: Killed by one, ready to feed hundreds. Those shapes, they weren't the largest. There was bigger, overhead. Circling. A shape that had been seen and reported on by just a few. A creature known to be elusive, yet also doubted in its existence.

The black shape did a sudden turn in the water overhead and - in a quick movement with shocking agility for something of its size - it lunged down to the body and passed in just the blink of an eye, kicking up sand from the loch's floor and temporarily blinding all. By the time the sands had settled, the top half of Mary's body was gone. By the time the sands had settled... The little fish were feasting again and by morning... *By morning the loveable author would have once again deleted every fucking word he had written in this lacklustre story, while simultaneously wishing a giant cartoon piano would just drop out of the fucking sky and squash his miserable existence.*

Whilst resisting the urge to just throw the fucking thing across the room, Reece slammed the lid of his computer down and promptly moved away from his desk. All evening he had been sitting there working and yet every damned sentence had been nothing but an unpleasant struggle.

Chapter Nine

Morning. Hardly a surprise; it was raining outside. Reece was tired, miserable and sitting in the hotel's "restaurant" area, looking down at his uninspiring breakfast.

At this stage, Reece didn't know what was more laughable; the restaurant itself, or the "food" that they served. With regards to the room, it was fairly small with about twenty or so tables. Around each of the tables, there were four plastic chairs - similar to those found in school cafeterias, back when he used to go to school that is. And the food?

Along the side of the wall there was a long sideboard. Resting on that, there were cartons of cereals that a person would find in kids' variety packs. Small cartons with a sign telling guests to help themselves to one. At one end of the breakfast "bar", there were jugs of orange juice (not freshly squeezed, going by the concentrated taste) and jugs of milk. Signs in front of the milk jugs stated whether they were skinned, or semi-skinned. Whatever they were supposed to be, given the lack of ice-buckets or refrigerating units, they were lukewarm. Unwilling to risk stomach cramps, Reece's breakfast consisted of cheap orange juice and dry cornflakes.

Weirdly, the reviews online made mention of there being a decent English breakfast to be had but, apparently that was "pre-covid", according to the lady who'd shown him to a seat. *Everything's covid-safe now so we have cereal.* Yet, the prices remained the same.

Reece's mood towards breakfast, and the day in general, might have been better had it not been for how tired he'd felt. He'd spent the night tossing and turning, frustrated at the lack of progress on the book. He always got like that when the writing didn't go to plan. Just *one* of the reasons why his wife divorced him. Still, he'd come here to write, and he wouldn't let his lack of progress deter him from continuing to try and - as such - he had his notebook and pen with him, just in case inspiration hit unexpectedly.

'Morning,' the *front of house* lady said.

Reece looked up, expecting to see another disappointed guest coming into the restaurant for their crappy breakfast. Instead, he saw the woman was talking to Lily, who'd just come through the front doors. In response to the woman, Lily smiled. Reece couldn't help but think she looked tired too. Clearly had a busy night.

'Oi,' Reece called out.

Both the woman at the front and Lily looked over.

'Given the lack of room upgrade, at least tell me this is free because it definitely isn't worth what the prices are currently set at.'

The woman looked genuinely insulted but Lily just laughed. She came over to say "hello".

'That is the upgrade,' Lily said. 'Previously it used to just be bread and butter. Before that,' she continued, 'it was just bread. Those were dark days indeed.'

'You have an answer for everything?'

Lily smiled. 'Usually.' Before Reece had a chance for a comeback, Lily's smile faded from her face as her expression changed back to one of a more serious nature.

Reece couldn't help but to comment, 'You look like you've had the same sort of night as me.' His comment brought Lily's smile back temporarily as she suddenly imagined him being bent over the hood of a police car, and roughly taken whilst also being cuffed. 'Everything good or did you stay in one of this place's beds as well?'

Again, Lily laughed. She wasn't ready to tell a stranger about her personal life though, even if he could make her smile. So, she said, 'I'm fine.' For the first time since walking into the restaurant area, she appeared to suddenly notice that it wasn't as busy as she had been expecting. She asked, 'Has it always been this quiet in here?'

'Since when I came in, yeah.'

'You scaring our patrons away with your sunny dis-position?'

'Or your menu is scaring them away. Probably a greasy-burger van down the road making a roaring trade.'

Not in the mood for an argument, Lily asked, 'How's the book coming along?'

'It's coming,' Reece said. Just as she wasn't willing to share too much with him, he wasn't looking to tell her all his worries and strifes either. And there *were* worries. He knew a book on Loch Ness would get a good number of sales. Nessie was a popular subject matter, even with people giving evidence to prove there was no such thing. He knew a number of Scottish people held the myth close to their heart. So, he wanted to do a *good* story for them. Well, a good story for them and the mar-ketplace as he really needed this one to be a success. One more flop and he knew, chances were, his agents would probably give up on him. Reece continued, 'I'm hoping the people will like it.'

'I'm sure they will,' Lily said, unaware what his writing was like on the best of days, let alone what he was actually writing now. She asked, 'And what about Lily the character?'

Reece smiled. 'Ah well she's a fish person.'

'I'm sorry - what?'

'A fish person.' If only as a way to both wind her up and test a Scottish person's reaction, Reece explained, 'Years ago the Pict people who used to live in these areas moved to the waters. They evolved to live there, growing gills... Occasionally they would come out to feed on people who walked too close to the water's edge. Lily is one of them. A slimy, smelly fish person.' He smiled. Lily didn't.

'Fish people?'

'Yep.'

'It sounds like you're writing a book about mer-men, not our Nessie.'

'I'm giving people something new to think about.'

'Something new?'

'Yeah. They know about Nessie. People have stepped forward and come up with various suggestions as to what "Nessie" could be… Such as a giant eel, right?'

'Sure.'

'Well, the mystery is more or less gone, isn't it?'

'Don't underestimate people's fascination with the Loch Ness monster.'

'I'm not. But I'm also giving them something new.'

'Fish people.'

Reece laughed. 'Fish people.'

'And you think that will sell well?'

'I'm hoping it will.' Reece could see from her expression that Lily was far from impressed with what he was saying. A proper sign that he should stop even trying to write this story and have a complete re-think instead. Although, for now, he was enjoying winding up Lily too much. He continued, 'I could do a sequel.'

'A sequel now too?'

'Yeah. I could have the Fish people fighting Nessie.'

'Like Godzilla and King Kong?'

'On a smaller scale and set in Loch Ness but, sure, why not? People love a monster movie, right?'

'I was thinking Lily the character was going to be a bit more glamorous,' she said.

Reece smiled again. 'And I was thinking about a room upgrade, or free - potentially better - breakfasts.'

Lily shrugged. 'So, we're both disappointed?'

'Would appear so.' Reece paused a moment and asked, 'Did I mention the fact that Lily the character has a penis?'

Lily laughed. 'And on that note,' she said, 'I must get over to my station so my colleague can go home for the day.' She looked at the soggy cornflakes in his bowl and said, 'Enjoy your breakfast.'

'Thank you. And, must say, looking forward to what-ever is microwaved for me at dinner time.'

Chapter Ten

Lily walked over to the front desk. Her colleague, Nicole James, was standing behind the desk - watching her on the whole walk over with a disapproving look on her face. It was a look which Lily couldn't help but to notice.

'What?' Lily asked.

'What do you mean, *what*? You're late and I'm just standing here watching you chat to one of the guests.'

'He called me over!'

'Sure he did.'

Lily shook her head at how grumpy her colleague was. The pair of them had never really seen eye to eye since Lily first started. As a result, the manager did his best to ensure they worked on opposite shifts. That way, he didn't have to deal with the drama.

Lily set her bag behind the counter and hung her jacket up on a nearby peg. 'Anything I need to know?' She looked at the computer and noticed that some of the previous day's guests had already checked out. 'How come these people have left already? They only arrived yesterday?'

'They came for the story, got what they need and left again. Not much to tell really, is there? These day's what happens down at the water is considered light enter-tainment and with the world going the way it is… Not much room for that sort of news now, is there?'

'Light entertainment? Not sure Jim would consider it that given it was his wife they found floating down there.'

Nicole laughed. 'Knowing Jim, he's probably the one that went around telling the reporters it was nothing more than light entertainment. I can hear him saying, it's no biggie. Can't you?'

Jim did appear to have a flippant way about him.

'Even so,' Lily said, 'you'd think they would have hung around to see if anything else was going to surface.'

'More interested in reporting about the latest government figures for the corona virus,' Nicole said. The added, 'Or whether Russia is going to invade Ukraine… Honestly, those Russians just need to fuck off.' She shook her head and got off the subject before she wound herself up to a point it ruined the rest of the day. She said, 'I think it's fair to say Nessie isn't going to bring the tourists back just yet. Bottom line is, too many people have said she doesn't exist now and the body that was found was a local person so… They'll probably go away and make up their own little stories to wrap it all up. Or, more likely, they'll just let the story fade.'

Lily noticed something else on the screen. 'Cancellations too?'

'Yep. A fair few. Check the reason given…'

Lily clicked through to the relevant screen. The majority of the reasons being given, for cancelling the room, were down to the travellers not being comfortable to travel yet. For the past two years, since the corona virus reared its ugly head, that's pretty much the only reason people gave for cancelling their rooms. But then, why would they say anything else when the virus was a "get out of jail free" card for being able to cancel things without fear of cancellation fees.

Lily sighed. When she'd gone home, the hotel was booked solid for a couple of weeks. Now it was back to being patchy. Whilst it was good they still had bookings, it wasn't *great* because the hotel was still in financial troubles thanks to the government previously closing all hotels down for a number of months. The manager, James Seamone, had already warned they might face redundancies unless there was a big turnaround; pretty much what every other local business was saying too.

The body washing up on the banks of Ness was *supposed* to have been their big turnaround point. A way of enticing the monster-hunters and press to come fill their hotels, book out the restaurants and shop in the local stores. Clearly the plan wasn't the success Mark Flemmich and Steve Chappo had been championing at the meeting last night.

'Maybe we'll get more bookings come in today?' Lily asked.

Nicole shrugged. She grabbed her coat and threw it on before hooking her car keys from her pocket. 'Not my problem. All I want now is my bed.' Whilst she wasn't exactly friends with Lily, she wasn't rude either and - so - on the way out, she said, 'Have a good day.'

Lily said nothing as she stared at the cancelled bookings. She glanced up and across the foyer, into the restaurant. Reece was sitting there still, staring out of the window to the rainy day outside. He looked lost in deep thought as he - obviously - continued working on his story. Occasionally, he'd make a note down on the pad before him - not that Lily could see what this was. She couldn't help but think that maybe he was the key to getting people back? It had been a while since a good story came about based on Nessie. In fact, she couldn't recall the last. Maybe if he managed to write something truly spectacular, it would reignite the world's fascination with the loch. It wasn't much but, at least there was a little hope.

Lily watched him for a while longer, curious to know what the man was dreaming up.

Chapter One (take 3)

As Nicole left the hotel, she pulled her jacket up over her head in an effort to stop the rain from soaking her recently washed hair. In further effort to stop from getting a soaking, she ran towards where she'd parked her car. As was often the way, it was parked at the furthest point away from the hotel's entrance as per the hotel's policy. *The guests get the decent spots, the workers get what is left.*

Knowing it was raining outside, she had already grabbed her keys in preparation to unlock her car. The less time she stood out in the open, the better, especially with the cold bitter wind blowing through. *Just another day in Paradise.*

As Nicole slid the key into the car's lock, she froze at the sound of a woman screaming from across the road, down by the water. She looked in the direction the scream came from but saw nothing. As she questioned whether she'd heard anything in the first place, another scream carried through the air.

Nicole called out, 'Hello?'

The response: *A woman screamed*.

Nicole cast a glance back towards the hotel, unsure as to whether anyone else was standing out in the carpark, or close to the entrance, who might have heard the cries but - she was alone. She turned back in the direction the screams had come.

'Hello?'

The only sound was the rain beating down on the sopping wet concrete. A little in the distance, she could hear heavy-droplets splashing into the loch. No more screams. For a split second, she convinced herself that she was hearing things. She twisted the key in the lock and - with the car now unlocked - pulled the door open.

Before she had a chance to sit in the dry, another scream echoed up from down by the water. She hadn't been hearing things.

Nicole closed the car door and started walking in the direction of the sound. In her mind, she was picturing someone injured, just clear of the road. Perhaps they'd slipped down the embankment and twisted their ankle awkwardly, she thought. Unable to get up, or pull themselves up the muddy sides, all they could do was scream.

'Hello? Is anyone there?' Nicole called.

She cast a quick glance up and down the road to check for traffic. When there was none to be seen, she hurried over - closer to the embankment leading down, through the trees, to the water.

Instead of just calling out *hello* again, Nicole asked, 'Where are you?' With any luck the person would scream out again, giving her a clue as to what direction to start searching in but - there was no response.

At the top of the embankment, Nicole stood. She was waiting, listening. Her heart was racing at the thought of someone lying close-by, hurt.

'Hello?'

The rain beating down.

The wind, pushing through overhead leaves hanging from their branches.

Crunching.

Crunching?

Nicole followed the alien-sound. Crunching, chewing. Wet slop slipping around. Sounds she recognised from growing up and sitting opposite her grandfather as he tried to eat food without his false teeth in. She used to watch the soft mush go round and round and round in his mouth, dribbling down the sides. She'd hear the wetness of the paste mushing up to something more akin to a liquid. It repulsed her before but now, these similar sounds - they filled her with a sense of dread instead. She knew she should just turn and run. Get in the car, drive home and forget about this or - go to the hotel and tell people what she'd heard. Let them call the police. Let *them* deal with it. Yet, her feet wouldn't stop.

She didn't call out again. Nicole knew there was no point. She continued following the noise, still with her heart racing at an uncomfortable level. A further worry that she was about to have a heart attack, even though she knew that wasn't the case. *Active brain…*

Ahead of her, there was a large thicket which separated Nicole from the water. The sound was coming from directly behind it. She walked closer to it and then froze on the spot. Her eyes widened. Her heart skipped a beat before racing once again. She held her breath so as not to be heard. There, on the other side of the bush… The monster, never before seen by her in anything but pictures, fed.

Slowly and quietly, Nicole reached into the inside of her jacket pocket. Her mobile phone. With a shaking hand, numb from cold, she pulled it out and turned the camera towards the bush. She was about to press the button when, from behind, a woman spoke.

'What are you doing?'

Startled, Nicole couldn't help but to scream. She spun on the spot and screamed again at the sight of Jennifer Brooks standing a few feet away. The woman's face was splattered red and her clothes were saturated in gore. Her hands, also red - like they had been dipped in a tin of the reddest of paints.

Jennifer asked again, 'What are you doing?'

Nicole just stood there - still with the sound of crunching coming from behind the bushes. She didn't know what to do, or say.

'I hope you aren't trying to record her,' Jennifer said with a disapproving tone about her voice. 'She doesn't like to be filmed.' In this light, the grey skies above, Jennifer's eyes looked almost jet-black. Weirder, with the faraway look upon her gaunt face, it looked as though she was staring straight through Nicole, as though she was nothing.

'Are you recording him?' Jennifer asked.

'No. I was…' Nicole thought on her feet but no excuses came to mind. Jennifer shook her head from side to side, accompanied with a "tutting" noise from the back of her throat.

'What are we going to do with you?' Without waiting for an answer, Jennifer reached behind her back and pulled out a large kitchen knife. She chuckled. 'Fish bait, I expect.'

Nicole ran to the side in a desperate attempt to get away from both the *thing* behind the bushes and the crazy woman standing so close. The moment she started to run, Jennifer cackled with joy and gave chase and…. Suddenly the author turned the legend of Loch Ness into a slasher story; the tale of a weird, old woman - both withered and witch-like in appearance - who'd feed the creature with people she murdered, whilst also helping to keep the monster from the public eye.

Chapter Eleven

Reece closed his notebook and laughed to himself as he put the lid back on his pen. The Fish People story idea might have been more original, albeit potentially offensive to the Scottish people in re-writing what happened to the Pict people, but, he could have had a lot more fun with the story of Jennifer Brooks and her care regime for Nessie. Although, that didn't necessarily mean the readers would have had more fun with either of the options.

'This shouldn't be that hard,' Reece said grimly. He watched through the window as Nicole got in her car and headed off to wherever she was going next. In the real world, she gets to live another day. In the fictional world, running round Reece's head, she'd probably have died within the next page or so; a meaty knife imbedded in her spine before Jennifer proceeded to gut her like a fish.

Despite hating the idea of the old woman feeding Nessie, which kind of reminded him of the film *Lake Placid* - where an old woman fed the giant crocodile, Reece did like the idea of Jennifer Brooks stabbing someone in the spine. In his head, he could envision her paralysing the victim and then really taking her sweet time in cutting bits away from her whilst the victim laid there, unable to do anything but suffer through the ordeal. It was sadistic for sure, but that just meant the audience would lap it up.

Before he forgot the idea, he opened his book and made a quick note of it. If it wasn't good enough for this book, it didn't mean it wouldn't be suitable for another. Shame to waste such an idea.

Once the note was written, he closed his book and - again - returned the lid to the pen. He got up from his chair, downed the last of his orange juice and started to make his way back up to his room. With the weather so bad outside, he hadn't yet decided what he was going to do with his day but, he didn't relish the idea of sitting in the "restaurant" all day, or the cramped room.

Lily watched as Reece walked towards the elevator. A small part of her was disappointed that he didn't stop to give her grief about the food, or room, like he had done every other time he'd seen her. She went to call out - a cheeky hope that he enjoyed his breakfast - but was stopped by the sound of her manager, James Seamone.

'Lily. Got a minute?' he asked.

Lily turned to face him. 'Sure.' She already knew from his tone that it wasn't going to be a "good" minute.

'Great. Ryan's coming down to cover. When he does, can you come to my office?'

The look on his face just reinforced that belief.

Lily asked, half-joking and half-serious, 'Should I be worried?'

'I'll be waiting,' James said as he made his way back down the foyer, to where his small office was tucked away in the far corner.

Without any acknowledgement of the question she'd just asked, Lily instantly started to question herself; had she done something wrong recently? She frowned. Not to her knowledge. Had the cash desk been missing money? Had something been misfiled? Had a customer smiled to her face but complained behind her back?

'Alright...' Ryan said as he came over to the desk. 'What's all this about?' he asked. Ryan was usually hidden away from the front of house due to his lacking people skills so, for him, this was a "treat" to be up front, away from the more manual labour reserved for him out back.

'No idea,' Lily said as her mind still supplied possible reasons for being summoned to the manager's office. If only to save face and appear unbothered, she said, 'Maybe he's giving me a pay-rise?'

Ryan laughed. 'Been sucking his dick recently then?'

'Yeah. No.' She pulled a face as she imagined going through with the act she'd been accused of. 'Gross,' she muttered.

'Well, fuck off. Take your time. It's nice to be able to sit back and put my feet up for a bit. See how easy you bastards have got it up here.'

'Yeah, okay then,' Lily said with a roll of her eyes. With nothing else to say, she made her way to the manager's office and whatever bullshit was waiting for her.

Chapter Twelve

'Take a seat,' James said.

Lily sat opposite him. He was one side of his desk; she was the other. The desk itself was a mess. Pages of accounts scattered across it; confidential information she was sure yet, he didn't seem to care how "readable" it was to those who came to his office. There were also a few mugs too; half-drunk hot drinks which he'd been too busy to finish and too lazy to take back to the kitchens. He probably expected the cleaners to do it for him, as though they didn't have enough rooms to clean already.

'Yesterday.'

Lily resisted the urge to sing, *When all my troubles seemed so far away.*

'Everything looked at lot brighter yesterday,' James continued. The hotel was booked up, more bookings were coming through online. Looked like, finally, we might have been on our way back to where we used to be, before the virus shut things down.' He continued, 'Got to say, I couldn't help but think the plan on getting things moving again was a little extreme but, at the same time, I didn't want to lose everything my family had worked for either so…' He shrugged. 'Needs must.'

'Of course.' Lily added, 'At least we had a vote though… So, if the numbers hadn't been right then we would have found another way.'

James smiled. Her being summoned into the office was nothing to do with how their government had decided on reigniting interest in Nessie and he didn't want to get bogged down in that conversation. He was just highlighting that, whilst he thought things were about to improve… Overnight figures showed that wasn't going to be the case after all.

'This hotel has been in my family for generations,' he said.

'I know.' Lily had been given the full time-line history lesson when she accepted the job. Furthermore, she'd heard it again and again when James had been found boasting to guests about its heritage too. He spoke so proudly about it, and all he had done but - she always found it funny - the only thing he did was get born into the "right" family. It wasn't as though he had worked for any of this.

'I'm not going to be the one to lose it,' he said.

'Of course,' Lily said.

There was a pause between the two of them. In that moment, Lily saw on his face exactly where this conversation was heading.

'You're firing me?' she asked.

'Usually by now, because of where we are situated, our summer bookings have already come in with most rooms being taken. We're down by 80% because people are too worried about booking things up, in case the country gets locked down again. England opens, we stay shut. We're open? England is shut. It's a mess, even with this "lesser" variant, as the press is calling it. People are still scared or, flip-side to that, people are jumping on planes back to the Canary Islands, because all *those* restrictions have ended again.' He continued, 'News of Nessie came out yesterday. The body. Poor Angie... Before covid struck, we would have been booked solid for a year with people flocking to the scene but now? We had bookings coming in thick and fast yesterday and - by morning - more than half have cancelled.' He sighed. 'The plan failed. Truth be told, even if they spread more of Angie around out there... I don't think it will bring people back here. People don't want dead bodies. We can see that now. They didn't come to Loch Ness for that. They came here for scenery, peace and the legend that is Nessie. A bit of fun,' he said. 'Now we've taken that from people with this ill-conceived idea.'

Lily wasn't really paying any attention to him. Her mind was fixated on the one question she'd thrown back which, as of yet, he hadn't answered. She didn't need to know about the hotel, or why people came to visit, or that James now believed the "plan" to bring people back was more damaging than anything else. She just wanted the answer to the question which directly impacted *her*. 'Are you firing me?'

James nodded. 'I need to make cut-backs.'

'So who else is getting fired?' Lily asked.

James didn't answer her. He didn't say anything. He was just sitting there, looking at her now. *Judging* her.

'What?' she asked.

'Is it true you've been working the guests?'

His question came out of the blue and took Lily by surprise. 'Working the guests. In what way?' She didn't need him to answer that. She knew what he was referring to. He wanted to know if she had gone back to her old ways - *fucking for cash.*

She answered him, 'No. It isn't true. Who told you that I was?' Again, another rhetorical question. She knew it would have been Nicole. The reason for their dislike for one another? Back when Lily, desperate for money, was whoring herself out to the local men - Nicole's partner just so happened to be one of her clients. It wasn't a one-time thing either. On a weekly basis, he would see her for one hour.

'I am not ashamed of my past,' Lily said. 'I did what I needed to. I did whatever it took to keep a roof over my head. That being said, it's my past. Sure, people might remember it… But the guests who come from out of town - they don't know what I used to do and it's not something I talk about so… It doesn't impact them and it doesn't reflect on your business; just as I promised you back when you gave me a chance too. I've kept my word. I've worked hard for you, even though the money is a *lot* less than what I used to earn on my back.' She said again, 'I'm not working the guests and I never have either. It just seems *some* people are too stuck in the past and talking shit to get you to fire me.' She asked again, 'So I am being fired because someone is talking lies behind my back?'

James smiled. 'Business isn't good. We were hoping it was picking up but, the simple truth of the matter is, it isn't. We need to make cutbacks.' Whether it was the truth or not, Lily knew this was nothing more than an excuse. James continued, 'We'll pay you until the end of the week...'

'Yeah? Fuck you.'

He paused a moment, unsure whether there was going to be any further abuse. When there wasn't, he continued, 'We will pay you until the end of the week but, it's probably for the best that you leave now, okay?'

There was so much Lily wanted to say in an effort to save her job but, she knew he had already made his mind up. She knew each word spoken would be nothing more than a waste of breath. She got up and walked towards the door before pausing a moment. Her words might not have saved her job but they would have made her feel better so, fuck it.

'I've worked hard for you. You can't say I haven't. I've left my past in the past, just as I promised. You might feel ashamed on my behalf, for what I used to do, but - I'm not ashamed and, even though it cost me my job now, I refuse to be. It's funny how I am the one who is considered dirty, untrustworthy and such - just because men used to pay me for sex, isn't it? No one ever thinks bad of the man who'd be paying; spending bill money on pussy because he is feeling horny. No one ever things the man is dirty for going girl to girl - some men even *begging* the ladies for unprotected sex. Nope. The men are *all* good. The girls though… Dirty skanks, aren't we?'

She turned back and looked at James. He said nothing. He wasn't even looking at her anymore. He was scanning the figures on the sheets in front of him. Lily shook her head.

'Fuck you,' she said again. With that, she took in a deep breath and used it to regain her composure. Then, she left the room - purposefully leaving his office door open as she did so.

* * * * *

Lily stormed across the foyer back to the reception desk. Ryan noticed her and immediately looked disappointed as, without knowing why she was called into the office, he expected he'd be heading back upstairs to carry on with his other tasks.

'Decent pay rise?' he asked.

'Fuck you,' Lily said as she grabbed her coat from behind the counter.

'That's a no then, I take it.'

Without stopping to pass the time with him, or explain what was going on, she stormed towards the exit.

'Where are you going?' he called out.

Lily stopped in her tracks. She turned to him, hate in her eyes. 'Like you don't already know!'

'Know what?'

'Everyone around here knows everyone's business, don't they? It's always been like that. No matter if you're trying to live a quiet life, or not. People are always there, sticking their noses in. Gossiping their shit and spreading their lies…'

'Lily, I have no idea what you're talking about.' He asked, 'Are you okay?'

'Fuck you! In fact - fuck all of you. Fuck this whole place!' She stopped for a moment as a thought struck her. As the thought further cemented itself in her head, she smiled. Then, she said again, 'Fuck all of you.'

Chapter Thirteen

Reece looked at his reflection, in the mirror of his rented room, as he did his raincoat up. With the rain hammering on the window, he couldn't help but look at himself and mentally call himself an *idiot*. Why? Rewind a couple of months and he had been standing in a shop which sold cheap anoraks. At the time he knew they'd be pretty shit in poor weather but, living in the south of the UK, it never got *that* bad. He knew this jacket wouldn't do much to keep him dry or warm in *this* weather. Yet the one he'd seen in the other store? Three times the price but promised protection against most. With the coat done up he looked himself up and down and, again, shook his head. *Idiot*. All to save a few pounds.

'Fuck it… If I catch my death of cold, saves the stress of having to finish the book.' He laughed, also aware that his death would probably turn his other books into best-sellers. The joys of an author; struggle in life only to find success and appreciation in death, where it becomes impossible to enjoy the royalties. 'Ah well,' he muttered. He'd get a drenching out there, but it was still better than sitting in the cramped room for another day.

Reece grabbed his phone from the side and slid it into the left-hand pocket of his jeans. He grabbed the room key and put that in his right pocket and then, turned for the door. He grabbed the handle and pulled the door open, only to visibly jump when he saw Lily standing there.

'Scared the shit out of me,' he said as he grabbed his chest. Lily didn't say anything. He noticed the look on her face; a pissed off expression and tears in her eyes. It was hard to tell if she was angry, or sad. 'You okay?'

'Can I come in?'

'Erm. Sure.'

Reece stepped back and held the door open for her. Lily entered and walked by him. He leaned out, into the corridor, to see if anyone was out there watching. A thought that, perhaps, he was about to be pranked, or something. The corridor was empty.

Reece closed the door. He turned to Lily who was standing on the far side of the room, looking out into the carpark below.

Unsure what to say, Reece tried to make a joke, 'Have you brought me something to eat to make up for the breakfast?'

Lily said nothing.

'Or maybe you're here to tell me another room is being set up for me and, you're going to tell me how grand it is...'

Lily continued to stare out to the world beyond. Despite how it looked, she wasn't just staring at the carpark. She was picturing the Scottish lands which laid beyond too. Along with the pictures, clips of her life played back, showing all the miserable years she had spent here. Quietly, she said, 'I hate this place.'

Reece wasn't sure whether he was supposed to chime in and tell her he felt the same. He said nothing.

Lily continued, 'I don't know why people would come here for anything other than to try and see the monster.' She added, 'All these hotels and little boutique shops and such would have shut down long ago if it weren't for the draw our Nessie has for tourists.'

Reece paused a moment and then asked, 'Is this your way of telling me the Fish people story isn't going to be good for you, or my sales? That I should write something more "Nessie-like"?'

Lily momentarily flashed a smile. She said, 'I'm not sure how well Fish people merchandise would sell compared to the cute teddies we're already shipping.'

'To be honest, I was thinking you could sell both sorts of merchandise, you know? I can already see a whole range of action figures and new toys for the traditional monster too. As a kid, I would have collected them all for sure. Definitely would have had the Fish people fighting the monster... Although in my story I'm thinking the Fish people are bad for *us*... I'm thinking they could be considering the good guys compared to Nessie, you know? Have to battle her to try and save their people from being eaten up.' He laughed. 'I should be writing this down.'

Lily changed the subject, 'I can take you somewhere.'

'Oh?'

'The perfect spot where you'll be able to find real inspiration for your story. And,' she continued, 'trust me... It will be a story relevant to Loch Ness, and something most people will never have heard of before.'

'That a fact?'

'But there's something I want from you.'

Reece laughed. There was always a catch. 'So let me get this straight; you're going to "give me a story idea" in exchange for something? Well, okay, what is it that I'm supposed to give you? Credit? Money? I mean I can do credit but money? I'm afraid you're barking up the wrong tree on that front...'

'I have savings. I don't need your money.' She casually said, 'I want you to get me out of here. One way trip back to wherever you live. Point me in the direction of a cheap hotel and I'll worry about myself from there.' She said again, 'I want you to get me out of here.'

Reece frowned. 'You want a lift back to the South of England?' He thought for a moment and then shrugged. 'Sure.'

'But,' she said, 'we have to go today because once I tell you the story idea...'

Reece couldn't help but to think this was all just a joke so he butted in with, 'Nessie will come and get you?'

Lily looked at him. In that moment Reece could see that she was more than serious. She almost appeared scared. She said, '*They* will come for me. And possibly you too, if they hear that you know.'

'Know what?'

'If you could give me a lift to my place, I'll pack a bag of essentials now. Then I'll take you to the spot and tell you everything.'

'Why don't you just tell me now? I've already said I'll give you a lift. For all I know you don't have a story and are just stalling for time whilst conning me out of a lift.'

'Conning you out of a lift? It's not exactly a con, is it? You'd already be driving that way. The only difference is, I'll be in your car with you.'

Well, when she put it like that.

'So, we have to go now?'

She nodded. 'If they know we're talking…' She didn't finish the sentence. Instead, she said, 'We have to go now.'

Reece looked around the small room. It wasn't exactly a hardship, having to leave early. He said, 'I'm presuming I don't get a refund because I leave early?'

From the look on her face, Lily gave him the answer he'd already expected. Still, it was worth a shot.

124

'Well okay,' Reece said. 'Give me a few minutes to pack up, yeah?'

Lily sat on the edge of the bed. 'I can wait.' Reece stood there a moment, unsure if she was joking and was about to leave him to pack. When he realised she was actually going to wait there, he started to gather his belongings. The whole time, he couldn't help but wonder what was going on in Lily's head. This girl was a far cry from the cheeky lass who'd checked him in the day before. Whatever it was, he also hoped that it would help with his story because - so far - he wanted nothing more than to take his notebook and pen and lob them both in the fucking loch. He was regretting coming here but, little did he know, in a few hours - he would come to regret even knowing Loch Ness, and the people here, existed in the first place.

Chapter Fourteen

'You'd best be directing me,' Reece warned Lily as they drove away from the hotel. They'd been driving for about five minutes now and whilst the road didn't exactly have many options with directions they could travel in, Lily hadn't shown any signs of being forthcoming with the route.

'Just keep going,' she said.

Not being that confident in taking his eye off the road, Reece cast her a quick glance. She was sitting in the passenger seat, staring out of the window. She had a far-away look on her face; lost in deep thought but about "what", Reece had no idea. He wanted to ask her why the sudden desire to get away from the area but - from the way she was talking - he'd already guessed she probably wouldn't tell him. If she did say something, it would probably not have been the whole truth anyway.

'Say what you want about this place though,' Reece said - if only to break the awkward silence, 'it sure is pretty.'

'Looks can be deceiving,' Lily said coldly.

Again, Reece couldn't help but to frown. All he could think was that something major must have happened in the short time she'd been at the reception counter and he'd been back up in his room. Her mood was *definitely* darker than when she'd popped into the restaurant to see him. He shrugged it off as possible "boyfriend trouble". Thinking back to his own life, relationships had always been one of the quickest things to sour his own mood so, it made sense. Even so, she had asked for a lift home and then for a lift back down south with him. He couldn't help but hope her mood would clear up before they started *that* long drive, otherwise it was just going to make an unpleasant journey seem even longer than it already was.

Just so she knew what was going on in his mind, he asked her, 'You going to be this quiet on the way down south? Just, if you are, it would be nice to know. Gives me some time to download some music for the ride, while you're packing up your bag.'

Lily didn't take the hint. 'I'll be fine.'

The shortness of her reply; Reece couldn't help but to laugh to himself. Unable to take the silence anymore, he leaned down and turned the radio on. *The Proclaimers* played which only made Reece laugh again. 'Guess you hear these guys all the time, huh?'

Lily didn't answer him. Reece took that as a "yes".

Chapter Two

Lily burst through her front door which such speed that the door swung wide open and slammed into the wall, denting the plaster. She didn't care. She'd lost the chance of getting her security deposit long ago and, even if she hadn't, the money owing was the last thing on her mind right now. All she cared about now was getting the hell out of Dodge.

She hurried down the hallway and into her bedroom. In there, she dashed to her wardrobe where she grabbed her overnight bag. Although, in this instance, it was less an "overnight" bag and more of a "never-fucking-coming-back" bag.

Lily had no idea who the old woman was that she'd seen down by the water. She hadn't recognised her and was trying as hard as she could to just forget what she'd seen. *She killed her. The old fucking woman killed her.* Lily had only been out and about for a walk. The ironic thing was, she rarely bothered venturing down to the loch as it was. Exercise wasn't really her thing but, with mounting bills and a need to just "get out", she'd gone down there to clear her head so as to try and formulate a plan for her future. Of all the days to go down there. Of all the paths she could have taken… *She killed her. The old fucking woman had killed her.*

Lily had gasped in shock when she had seen it happen - this woman so viciously thrusting a knife into the back of the other woman. It wasn't the loudest of noises, especially as it was mostly drowned out by the victim's scream of pain and yet - the old woman had still managed to hear her! Her gaze snapped straight to her as Lily just stood there, a look of shock and horror on her own face. There was no guilt in the woman's expression.

There was no concern that she'd been seen. Instead, she just laughed. Except, it was less a "laugh" and more a "cackle". Then she raised a bloody hand and pointed a bloody finger straight at Lily. She screamed, 'I know who you are!'

Lily didn't recognise her and nor did she want to know where this murderer knew her from either. She just wanted to get out of there. That was when she turned and ran, back down the muddy "path" she'd been coming down initially. The woman screamed and yelled and laughed… She called out warning that there was no place Lily could run. There was no safe place where she couldn't be found and that - by running - she was only delaying the inevitable. Lily didn't care. She ran, and she ran as fast as her legs could carry her. What's more, she didn't stop.

Lily was in her bedroom throwing clothes into her overnight bag, along with a few of her more prized possessions that she couldn't live without. Nothing much, just jewellery which had been handed down by her long-dead mother, her expired passport and what little money she had in the apartment. There certainly wasn't enough to start a new life elsewhere but, she didn't care. It was enough to get out of there for now. Enough to find somewhere else to stay before she contacted the police and tell them what she had seen down by the water.

As she continued stuffing clothes into her bag, a sickness swirled in her stomach. For a split-second Lily hoped that it was just nerves and nothing more but, then, she bent over and threw up over her carpet. Nerves, fear, stress; a puddle of putrid emotion splashed on the carpet and soaking into the fabric where it would leave a grim stink of stomach bile. *Definitely goodbye "security deposit"*. As soon as she stopped vomiting, she stood up straight and wiped her mouth clean with the back of her hand. Her stomach was still dancing, as were all the different emotions, but it didn't feel as though she was going to vomit again. She tried to dismiss the unpleasant and uncomfortable feelings as she got back to packing her clothes.

Lily didn't stop to check what outfits she was packing. She literally just threw anything in there until the bag was full. When it was, she did the zip up and hurried back out of the apartment. All in all, she must have been in there for less than ten minutes.

She didn't slow down as she ran down the corridor outside her apartment. Not even to greet her neighbour who was coming up the stairwell. She bounded down the stairs and straight out of the apartment block's foyer and into the carpark beyond. That was where the driver was waiting.

Her ride to salvation.

Chapter Fifteen

When Lily climbed into Reece's car, she couldn't help but laugh when he jumped. She put her bag down by her feet and closed the door before she asked, 'Are you okay?'

'Lost in my own world,' Reece said. He admitted, 'You actually scared the shit out of me.' As was often the way, he'd drifted into his own little book world, planning what he needed to be writing the next time he sat down at the computer. Whilst he didn't yet have a good enough idea for Nessie, he did like the idea of having a character running away from the area so - as long as he didn't forget it - that was a definite scene for his book. With the way she spoke to him when she got in the car - and with the way she was looking at him now -

he couldn't help but notice her mood had seemingly changed again. 'You seem in a better mood?'

'Sorry about earlier. I just wanted to get my stuff and hit the road.' She let out a sigh. 'Now I've got my stuff, I feel like I can relax a little bit, you know?'

'I guess,' he said. Reece leaned forward and turned the key in the car's ignition. The engine started with no issues and he leaned back in his seat again, before turning to Lily. 'So,' he said, 'where we headed?'

Lily frowned a moment and then asked, 'What are the people like down south?'

'What's the matter? Never been out of Scotland before?'

'Actually, no.'

'I was about to be shocked but, to be fair, I'd never been up here before now so… Guess we both need to get out a bit more, huh?'

Lily asked again, 'So what are the people like?'

'Same as everywhere else really. You get some nice people. You get some not-so-nice-people. You know, same old, same old.'

'Are they judgemental?'

Reece couldn't help but show his confusion at her question. Given he had no idea what the context this was being asked in, it was hard to answer. 'In what way would they be judgemental?'

'Like, if they found out you'd done something in your past that most people deem... disgusting...'

Reece laughed. 'Well now I'm curious. But to answer your question, your past is your past. So long as you're not hurting people... Most wouldn't give a shit but, you know... There's always some out there who look for any excuse to be able to look down their nose at someone. My advice? You meet those people, you just walk away. They're worth less than nothing.' He paused a moment and eyed her up and down.

'What?'

He laughed. 'Trying to figure out what you could have done that's so bad you're worried about how others would see you, if they were to find out.'

The sad truth of the matter was, if Lily left with Reece now then she knew her past would - once again - be her present. With no other way to support herself, she'd need to get money fast and the fastest way she knew was to sell herself. It wasn't ideal but, if it got her away from this life here and what these people were then - she'd have to go through with it.

If only to test the water, Lily said, 'I used to sell myself.'

'As in...'

'Prostitution.'

Reece thought for a moment. Then, he simply shrugged and said, 'Cool.'

Lily laughed. 'That's it?'

'What else am I supposed to say? Sorry, was I meant to be disgusted at that? It's your body. So long as it was your choice, as far as I am concerned you can do what you want. If we were friends and I found out, all I would ask is whether you're happy and being safe. Anything else and it's not my business. It's no one's business but your own.'

Lily didn't know what to say. She just smiled. A small hope that everyone down south thought the same way. A belief that this could well have been the difference between coming from a relatively small village, where everyone knew each other's business, and coming from a larger city. And to think, growing up, she'd always told herself that city life wasn't for her.

Lily faced forward and pointed. 'You want to head down this road…'

Reece nodded. 'Easy enough.' He asked, 'You going to tell me where we're headed yet?'

Lily simply replied, 'The birthplace of Nessie.'

Chapter Sixteen

Reece frowned as he pulled into what appeared to the carpark of the local town hall.

'Park anywhere,' Lily told him.

Reece didn't waste time. He turned into the nearest spot and, without taking time to park properly within the lines, he asked Lily, 'Is this the town hall?' It looks like it's the town hall.' He laughed. 'Nellie running for office?' He glanced over at Lily. 'Okay, why are we here?'

Lily didn't say anything. She got out of the car and closed the door. Reece laughed - but more out of confusion. Without moving from his seat, he looked all around - into the darkest corners of the carpark. A sudden concern he was about to be mugged. As far as he could tell, they were alone.

Reece climbed out of the car. 'Lily? Are you going to tell me why we're here?'

Lily was by the main entrance of the town hall. She was looking around, under the various rocks and flower-pots. Suddenly she let out a little squeal of delight. She bet down, grabbed a key and lifted it triumphantly.

'Seriously?' Reece couldn't hide his surprise. 'They keep the spare key somewhere so obvious? I thought it was only horror movies that did that? Surely anyone could come by and let themselves in?!'

'When you see inside,' Lily said, 'you'll realise there's not much that's worth stealing.'

'Vandals?'

'If vandals wanted to damage the property, do you think it would honestly make a difference if they had the key?'

It was a fair point.

Lily unlocked the front door. She pushed the door open and held it there. She turned and gestured Reece to come over.

'Seriously - what are we doing here? What is this place?'

'I already told you,' she said, referring back to when she'd said it was *the birthplace of Nessie*. 'I'll tell you everything,' she said. She walked into the property. The door closed behind her.

Reece gave another glance around. Still no one.

'Okay just so you know, I'm going to be really upset if there's a cult in there, waiting for me. People dedicated to making Nessie a reality, or whatever.' He was only half-joking but, having read a book called *Octopus*, he was also aware that his "joke" could have been based upon truth. With the sudden thought of the book in his head, he couldn't help but feel a little more apprehensive about heading in after Lily. It had all the hallmarks of a classic horror story right here: The pretty girl lures the dumb man into the trap. In the hope of getting his dick wet, he follows her. Another quick look around; the carpark was deserted, other than his own car. He muttered, 'Fuck it.'

With a sigh, he followed Lily. The more time he was spending with her, the more he was starting to wonder whether she was "okay". He walked into the building. The door closed behind him.

Chapter One

Lily was right; a quick look around the building and there was nothing of note that was worth stealing. There was a stage, no doubt used for amateur dramatics. There were plastic chairs, stacked tall against a far wall. There were painted posters tacked to the wall. Other than that - mainly dust and cobwebs with a heavy stink of disinfectant hanging in the air.

As Reece walked in, Lily was standing on the stage. She was facing him.

'Okay,' he said, 'are you going to explain why we're here now?'

For a moment, Lily looked unsure as to whether she was doing the right thing. The plan in her head was to confess everything that had happened within the community. Let him go and write about it in his book, paint it as truth and let the investigations bring everyone down. Meanwhile, she starts a new life elsewhere. They weren't going to let her move on with her life, they weren't going to let her forget her past. They'd never let her progress. If she wanted to make something of herself, she needed to do so elsewhere. And this was the start of that journey.

'This is getting stupid,' Reece said, clearly irritated that he was just standing there like a muppet whilst waiting for answers.

'Nessie never existed,' Lily said.

'Well, I don't think that is a surprise to anyone,' Reece said. 'Pretty much every scientist has said the same thing for the last ten years at least... And that's not much of a start for a new story based *on* Nessie...' He asked directly, 'Are you just trying to waste my time? For someone who wants a favour from me, that seems like a pretty weird way of getting me to help...'

'Nessie has and always been an invention of our own making. We made her up. The first sightings, subsequent sightings - where drug-fuelled hippies weren't involved at least... They were all made up to get tourism.' She laughed. 'You can see why they did it, can't you? It's not like we get too much good weather up here. We have nice scenery, sure, but you can get that in warmer climates too. They needed something else to entice people up here and, everyone loves a good monster story, right?'

Reece was just standing there. Really, there wasn't much to question about any of this. It was strange hearing all of this but, at the same time, it made some kind of sense. Researching other topics for other books, he had certainly heard weirder stories.

'And people just kept this story up for all these years?'

'Nessie is worth a lot of money to Scotland. It was a lie, sure, but it was a harmless lie. A bit of fun and mystery and...'

'Then someone died.'

'Whole of the country went to lockdown. A lot of our businesses rely on the tourism trade. We needed to do something to get people back and... A new story was invented to do just that.'

'You're telling me that someone signed this off? To have a person killed in order to make people believe Nessie was not only real, but also a man-eater? I can understand the hoax around the creature itself but, this takes that to another level entirely. Why are you even telling me this?'

'I don't think Angie was a one off.'

'Angie?'

'The woman whose body was found.' Lily said, 'I think they're going to keep looking for bodies to be found in an effort to try and get more people up here.' She paused a moment and then admitted, 'I think it won't be long before I'm one of them.'

'You?'

'They look at me like I'm less than pond scum because of what I did in the past. They won't let me progress. Every time I think I'm fitting in somewhere, making what they would consider a "proper" life for myself... Something happens, and I am knocked back down to square one. Every time. I'm nothing to these people so...'

'You think you're disposable.'

'And that's why I want you to drive me out of here. Then, go home and write your Nessie book but write *this* Nessie book... Expose them. Sure, people might consider it fiction but, the people who live here... They'll know... My little "fuck you" from me to them.'

Reece took a moment to take all this in. Even if she wasn't telling the truth, it still made for an interesting angle on an otherwise stale story. Everyone knew about the Loch Ness monster. Everyone had heard the stories and seen the pictures - all of which proven to be bullshit. This angle for the story though... This gave fresh insight into the hoax. What made it more interesting was the fact it didn't just reveal Nessie to be "fake"; it revealed a bigger monster lurking behind her. And if she was telling the truth, so what? It wasn't like the people could say anything, was it? If anything, it might make them *stop* having any more bodies wash up along the shores though.

'Say something,' Lily said. She was watching Reece, waiting for a reaction, desperate to hear what he had to say about everything. Still, he just stood there, like he'd run out of batteries and simply "switched off".

Reece shrugged. 'It's a good idea for a book?' More of a question than a statement. Honestly, he had no idea what he was supposed to say to her. If she spoke the truth, it was bad. If she was talking crap then… She was insane? Or, she had a good imagination and should re-train as an author? Unless, he thought, maybe that was what she was angling for? 'So, if I use that as a part of my story, am I supposed to pay you shares?'

'I just want a lift,' she said.

'You won't try and sue me later if I publish it?'

'Nothing is in writing. How could I sue you?'

A fair point; her word against his and it certainly wouldn't be the first time someone had tried to sue an author, claiming the published story was stolen.

'And this is real?' Reece asked, not that it *really* mattered either way.

'If it wasn't, why would I be asking to go with you? More to the point? Why would I be asking you to take me *now* and not at the end of your trip? I need to get out of here and now you know the truth...'

Reece couldn't help but to laugh. 'My life is in danger?'

'Yes.' Lily's face was so serious when she said it that Reece couldn't help but to laugh again. She cut to the chase and asked, 'Can we...' She froze.

'What?'

Lily was staring behind Reece. Slowly he turned around to see what had stolen her attention. Steve Chappo was standing in the doorway. He was grinning from ear to ear. He raised his hands and - with no immediate words - he started applauding.

'Now *that* is a story!' He laughed.

Chapter Two

'So you're the author?' Steve asked as he walked up to Reece.

'Steve, don't…' Lily warned him.

Steve looked at her with a confused look on his face. 'Don't want? What? Am I not allowed to talk to your friends? That's a bit selfish of you, is it not?'

'Please, just leave us alone…'

Steve shook his head and turned back to Reece who was just standing there, not really sure what was going on.

'Ignore her,' Steve said, 'she isn't all there.' He asked again, 'So you're the author she was telling me about?'

'Maybe,' Reece replied, unsure whether he was setting himself up for something.

'Here to write a book on Nessie?'

'Thinking about it.'

'Well, I hope it is better than some of the films people have released recently. They've been a fucking embarrassment. Did you see the one with Ted Danson? I kid you not, they did a film about Nessie and a family of baby fucking dinosaurs. I mean, get me a bucket. Pure vomit inducing trash.'

Reece laughed. 'Well, I hope my book is going to be better.'

'Stands a good chance if you use Lily's story.' He turned to Lily and said, 'That was a good story. I'm surprised you didn't try and write it for yourself. Could have been our resident author. Another reason for people to visit us.' Steve asked Reece, 'Did you like her story?'

'As a piece of fiction it could work.'

'That all you have to say?'

'Well, I'd be worried about dividing the audience. You know - some people would buy a book on the Loch Ness monster and expect to actually have a story based upon it. They might be upset if they ended up with a bunch of… I don't know… hillbillies?'

'Hillbillies?!' Steve laughed. 'Wouldn't be we High-land-billies?'

'That could work,' Reece said, as he laughed along with Steve.

'Any other notes for our would-be author? You saying her story won't work because it might anger some folk?'

'No. I'm saying it might divide the audience but then - good art usually does. So long as you have some people loving it and not everyone hating it. You're doing something right.'

'That a fact?'

'Sure. Why not? As for upsetting people with the story itself, well that's always a danger when you're trying something new but, it's not enough of a reason to shy away from it…'

Steve turned back to Lily and said, 'I hope you're listening to all of this. You're learning from a master!' He turned back to Reece and confessed, 'Although I'll be honest, I've not read your work before now... Am I missing anything good?'

Reece laughed. 'Not according to my reviews.'

'Well, that's saved me some time then, I guess.' Steve smiled and then, in the blink of an eye, he pulled a knife from his pocket and thrust it in the side of Reece's neck. Lily screamed as Steve pulled the blade out and Reece stumbled a few steps to the side with a jettison of blood spurting from the fresh wound and a shocked look on his face. He fell to the floor where his body soon went limp. Steve had already stopped watching him. With the artery severed so perfectly, he knew Reece wouldn't be a threat anymore. Instead, he had turned his attention directly to Lily who was just standing there, too afraid to move.

For a moment, the pair stood in silence as - on the floor - Reece breathed his last. Eventually Steve said,

'Did you honestly think I wouldn't follow you after you told me about him? Did you honestly think I would let you go off with someone else? I already told you, you're mine.'

'I'm sorry…'

'And it's a good job I followed you, given the story you spun. Do you honestly have any idea what a shitstorm that could have brought down on all of us here? Are you honestly that fucking selfish?' Steve shook his head disapprovingly. 'Honestly, I thought better of you than that. I'm actually disappointed.'

'I'm sorry…'

'But you're not though, are you? Had I not walked in here and caught you… Had I not done this… You wouldn't have been sorry at all. You would have left with him. You would have let him write the story. You would have left all of us to rot. No. You're only sorry because you were caught.' Steve sighed. 'I think you and I need to go for a little drive, don't we?'

Lily turned and ran off the side of the stage and out of the stage-door. Down the end of the long hallway, there was a fire escape. She just hoped that it would be un-locked, or - at the very least - with a key close to hand.

From the stage area, Steve laughed. 'Now where do you think you're going? Honestly… You're going to make me chase you?! No. You're okay. I'll wait here.' Steve didn't need to chase as he knew, Mark Flemmich was standing on the other side of the fire escape door, a hammer in hand and a stance with which to swing it.

Chapter Three

It was a peculiar, uncomfortable feeling to wake up to; the feeling of a man's fingers inside her pussy. Slowly Lily opened her eyes. The world pulled into focus although - when it did - she wished that it hadn't.

Lily was laying naked on a stone slab, surrounded by trees in all directions but one. In front of her there was a perfect "cut out" in the woodlands, showing the loch. Moonlight glistened from the eerily still waters. To her side, and more alarming to her than anything else, Mark Flemmich was standing there with a dirty grin on his face and two of his fingers jammed up in her cunt.

He wheezed with excitement as he spoke, 'Can feel why he would want to fuck you. Nice and tight up there.'

Lily tried to speak; to tell him to get off. Her mouth was gagged tightly. She writhed against the chain restraints which bound her down, hoping for enough movement to shake away from him. No such luck.

Steve called over from down by the water's edge, 'Well just keep in mind that you're probably scraping some of my cum out of her while you're doing that.' He laughed. 'Was only the other day I creamed up in her.'

'More flavour,' Mark said. As if to prove a point, he pulled his fingers from Lily's vagina and gave them a lick clean with his pointed tongue. 'Fishy,' he said. Lily closed her eyes and turned away from him; a wish that she could magically transport herself somewhere else. She couldn't.

'Don't worry,' Steve called over to Lily. 'All this will be over soon.' Lily opened her eyes and craned her head to see where Steve was. Mark was blocking her view -

still with that fucking smile on his face. Behind him though, Steve was throwing chunks of Reece into the water as bait. Steve continued, 'Sure she will be here soon...'

Panicked, Lily started to fight harder against the chains, not that they were going anywhere. Instead, the cold, hard metal dug into her wrists and made them bleed. Mark watched her, suitably bemused.

'Now why would you go and hurt yourself like that?' He leaned over her and pinned her in place to stop her writhing. His face up against hers. His rancid breath breathed directly up her nose. She stopped struggling as it was pointless to even try with his weight on her as well. She turned her head to the side to escape his obnoxious scent. 'That's better,' he said. 'Nice and calm... Don't want to frighten her, do we?'

From down in the water, there was a loud splash. Mark's eyes widened with excitement. Without saying anything, he quickly got off Lily. Having heard the noise, she opened her eyes and looked down to the sound of the splashing. The sight of the water rippling.

Steve had stepped back from the water's edge now, despite there being more of Reece ready to throw in should there have been the need to. Quietly, as if to himself, he said, 'She's here...' Then, with more excitement, 'She's fucking here!'

A few feet from the shore, a small dome shape came up from the water. Two red eyes appeared; staring forward and full of hunger. The monster's reptilian-like head pushed out of the water, on the end of an extended neck.

Mark and Steve both froze to their spot; fear and admiration. The creature pulled itself up, out of the water - two long flippers as arms, two long flippers as legs. It lurched up towards the stone slab, where Lily laid - chained, petrified.

Steve whispered, 'She's beautiful.'

A few grunts from its impressive throat but an otherwise quiet, hulking beast. Its mouth slightly open with

160

teeth so sharp on display. It snorted a spray of snot from the two nostrils close to its eyes as it leaned it's head down towards Lily. Lily held her breath and turned her head to the side, hopeful that the creature would turn away and look elsewhere for food.

Still Steve and Mark stood motionless, in awe of the creature. No matter how many times they came to this spot, to offer the sacrifices, the creature never got any less impressive to witness. The only frustrating thing being that they couldn't let the world see the beast for themselves. A knowledge that, if they really knew of its existence, they wouldn't come to just watch it. They'd come to hunt it, capture it and lock it away to study.

By feeding her in this way, she kept herself to herself - with the exception of the odd glimpse here and there. The occasional photos. Photos which a "team" of professionals were always on hand to quickly dismiss as "hoax". All these people playing a bigger part in keeping the real Nessie a secret, but also feeding the idea of her into the public consciousness to help with bringing

money into Scotland. It was a fine line they were dancing, but one which had been walked for many years
now.

'Go on, girl,' Steve quietly said as the creature lifted
its head up away from Lily. He had seen this before. The
first time, he thought their offering wasn't good enough
and that Nessie wasn't going to feast. He worried that
she was just going to turn back and pull herself back
into the water. His worry was short-lived when she
thrust her head back down to the victim, ripping out the
poor woman's jugular in a quick, vicious movement.
Tonight, would be the same. He encouraged her again,
'Go on, girl…'

Chapter Seventeen

Reece's agent closed the book. She set it down on the desk separating her and Reece. Reece was watching her with an excited look on his face.

'Well?' he asked.

His agent hesitated a moment. She took in a breath and asked, 'I have questions.'

'Okay.' Reece laughed. 'Hopefully I have answers.'

'The biggest surprise was that you killed yourself in the book.'

'Marketing gimmick.'

'Marketing gimmick?'

'Yes. Adds to the mystery.'

'How so?'

'We release the book as me, and my pen name.'

'I didn't realise you have a pen name…'

'No one does yet. And hopefully they won't. But if we release the book in both names, we can say that I never came back from the Scottish trip. That, in turn, lends to the belief that I was killed up there. It adds more weight to the story. Was I murdered up there by the good, old Scottish folk? Have I just stopped writing? Either way, it adds mystery, right? Also, if people think I am dead, it means they take another look at my older releases too… Like, if I was writing the truth in *this* book - what about my other books? Were there "truths" in there too, which could add another element to the story? People read them and go and investigate them for themselves. You know?' Like an excited kid, he continued, 'Anyway, I carry on working with you as the pen name author so, I'll still bringing money in. But, for all intents and purposes, the author Reece Walker is dead.'

The agent hesitated a moment. After a pause, she asked, 'And do you honestly think the Scottish people will be happy you're basically implying they invented the Loch Ness monster to bring in tourism?'

Mark shrugged. 'What does it matter to me? I'll be dead.' Then, to give a better answer, he said, 'Look - no one believes in Nessie anymore. Too many scientists have disproven her existence now. But if you think about it, if I release the book like this… It actually gives reasons as to why the scientists could be lying… I'm not saying the Scottish people invented Nessie if you read further into the book. I'm saying they know she is real but they're also keeping her a secret. Why? Because they know people will hunt her down. They'll stalk her. They'll kill her. Be it on purpose or not. *But…* They also need Nessie for tourism so, occasionally, they release stories about her to get people interested again, right? People get interested, people flock up there to see her for themselves… They never do. Meanwhile, their scientists come forward and call the pictures a hoax. People leave, deflated that she isn't real… Years later, when they need another boost to the economy… Nessie is shown to the public again… So, yeah, one part of the book says they invented her but the actual truth is, they're keeping her safe *whilst* making lies to bring in money for their economy. If you think about it, it's pretty clever…'

The agent smiled. 'I'm not sure it's as clever as you think it is.'

'It has fish people.'

'Again… Not sure it's as clever as you think it is.' She sighed and tapped her finger against the hardback cover. 'And none of these people exist?'

'None of them. All figments of my imagination. Can't get sued because I'm not calling anyone murderers.'

The agent sighed. 'Well I'm not sure but… Did you have a name to use?'

'As my pen name?' Reece smiled. 'One name pops to mind.'

'Care to let me in on it?'

Printed in Great Britain
by Amazon

60093905R00095